His voice had lost its caressing tone

Keri was puzzled. He'd answered her phone, and suddenly everything had changed.

"What's the matter? Is Robyn all right?" she asked.

He walked back toward her and said, "My sister's fine. The hospital says you're to collect her at noon." Then he handed Keri a piece of paper. "This was on your desk by the phone."

Confused, Keri stared at a check for a large sum of money, made out in her name. It carried Ben's printed signature and a counter-signature by Ben's brother, Rick. "You can't think I'd accept money from Rick," she said, knowing that was exactly what Ben did think.

"Why not?" he snarled, his anger obvious. "It wouldn't be the first time I've paid off one of his inamoratas."

Valerie Parv had a busy and successful career as a journalist and advertising copywriter before she began writing for Harlequin in 1982. She is an enthusiastic member of several Australian writers' organizations. Her many interests include her husband, her cat and the Australian environment. Her love of the land is a distinguishing feature in many of her books for Harlequin. She has recently written a colorful study in a nonfiction book titled *The Changing Face of Australia*. Her home is in New South Wales.

Books by Valerie Parv

HARLEQUIN ROMANCE
2693—MAN AND WIFE
2765—ASK ME NO QUESTIONS
2778—RETURN TO FARAWAY
2788—HEARTBREAK PLAINS
2797—BOSS OF YARRAKINA
2860—THE LOVE ARTIST
2896—MAN SHY
2909—SAPPHIRE NIGHTS
2934—SNOWY RIVER MAN
2969—CENTREFOLD

Crocodile Creek

Valerie Parv

Harlequin Books

TORONTO • NEW YORK • LONDON
AMSTERDAM • PARIS • SYDNEY • HAMBURG
STOCKHOLM • ATHENS • TOKYO • MILAN

Original hardcover edition published in 1988
by Mills & Boon Limited

ISBN 0-373-03005-3

Harlequin Romance first edition September 1989

For Paul and all the crocodiles

CHAPTER ONE

WAS she glad to be back? Keri Donovan let her gaze meander over the broad expanse of brown river as it wended its way through the paperbark swamps and flood plains. She searched for signs that the land had changed as much as she herself had, but found nothing. There was a world of difference between eighteen and twenty-four, but it was a mere speck in the aeons by which change was measured in the outback.

The spear grass which grew taller than a man had probably been burnt out a dozen times since she left, but its lushness gave no sign. Like the shapely lancewoods and Messmates crowding the water's edge, the grassland looked unchanged.

Across the river, a Jabiru skated over the surface of the water, building up sufficient speed to lift its heavy body and long legs into the air. Holding her breath, she willed the bird upwards, not releasing her breath until the Jabiru was safely airborne. It was a game she and Robyn had played as teenagers, as if their combined willpower could be transmitted to the struggling birds.

Above the drone of the mosquitoes came the whir and splash of the giant barramundi and the hoarse roar of a bull crocodile, a reminder that the Top End of Australia held its terrors as well as wonders. In spite of that, she was glad to be back. How could she have thought she could be happy living in a city, even Darwin?

Rolling the sleeves of her khaki shirt up above her elbows, she slathered mosquito repellent on to her arms. It hadn't taken long for her suntan to deepen, she noticed. What other changes could be taking place in her? She leaned out across the billabong and sought her reflection in the dark water, keeping her balance with a hand clamped around an outward-leaning tree trunk.

Staring back at her was an oval-shaped and strangely piquant face which looked greenish in reflection, where her usual skin tone was golden and glowing. The green tint made her look ethereal, an effect which was heightened by the halo of honey-coloured hair fluffing out around her head.

Foolishly aware of what she was doing, she smiled and the reflection smiled back. The effect was a startling mix of teenager and temptress, hardly the effect she wanted. She pulled back and shook out her hair, combing it with splayed fingers. It was just as well that there was no one around to see her. Smiling at her reflection, indeed!

But she *was* under observation, she realised as she felt a warning prickle between her shoulder blades. She spun around. 'Who's there?'

The swamp grass parted and a tall, wiry black man emerged. He was dressed in the khaki and denim near-uniform of a stockman. His teeth flashed whitely in his dark face. 'G'day, miss.'

'Good day. You startled me. I didn't know anyone was around.'

He held out a hand to her. 'It's me, Nugget, Miss

Keri. You don't remember me, do you?'

Her brows came together as she concentrated then her smile widened. 'Nugget! Of course. It's good to see you again. Are you still at Kinga Downs? What brings you to Casuarina?'

Her barrage of questions finally halted and he looked at the ground, shy in the face of her enthusiasm. 'I've been head stockman on Casuarina a long time. Since you left Kinga Downs I've been hoping you'd come back.'

Nugget had been a staunch friend when she was a regular visitor to Kinga Downs, the centre of the Champion cattle empire. Now he was head stockman at the outstation, Casuarina. She was pleased to see he had done so well. He had taught her much about bush lore and influenced her choice of career. As a teenager, he had been gangly with hands and feet seemingly too large for his wiry body. Now he had reached full manhood and he stood proud and tall, a modern man in his western clothes but still with the mysterious aura of the Stone Country about him. 'I've been away studying,' she explained. 'I'm a ranger now.'

He inspected her uniform. 'So I see. You're a proper-good ranger, too, I'll bet.'

She laughed. 'You always took my side, Nugget.'

'You needed somebody. You were so lost in the bush. But not any more, huh?'

'I hope not. I've learned a lot since I went away.' She perched on a lightning-blasted tree stump and crossed a slim ankle over her knee. 'What brings you out here, Nugget? Chasing stray stock?'

He pushed his bush hat far back on to his head

and scratched his forehead. 'We've been losing cattle for days. I'm betting a big kinga took 'em.'

'Big kinga?' she wondered aloud. 'You think a crocodile took your strays?'

He gestured towards the river, innocently quiescent under its blanket of waterlilies. 'You bet. There's maybe two big crocs in there. No good to swim. No room.'

To the native stockmen, 'no room' meant that the crocodiles had first claim to the waterhole. Knowing what the huge saurians could do to anyone who invaded their territory, she was happy to give them all the room they needed. 'I think you're right about two big crocs living in there.' She gestured towards the waterhole. 'They're the reason I'm here, to survey them for the Conservation Commission.'

His eyes widened at the endless kinds of craziness her people exhibited in this timeless land. 'You got a gun?' he demanded.

She shook her head. 'I won't need one. I'm here to observe and take photographs. I won't be doing any shooting.'

'Maybe I'd better stick around,' he said solemnly.

This was the last thing she wanted. Nugget Malone was one of Ben Champion's most valued and trusted men. His absence would bring questions and she didn't want it generally known that she was back. Robyn Champion knew she was here. It was for her sake that Keri had agreed to come. And because Robyn had assured her that Rick was safely married by now. Just thinking of Rick Champion chilled her blood. Not for any of the Champion men would she have returned to the scene of so many bitter memories.

The stockman's eyes on her brought her out of her reverie. 'Don't worry about me,' she assured him. 'My camp's up there on the high ground.'

He looked approving when she showed how she had made her camp more than sixty feet above the high-water mark, well clear of the mud slides made by the giant crocodiles. Her supplies swung from a tree, out of reach of wandering buffalos. 'You haven't forgotten what I taught you,' he said, his gravelly voice echoing his pleasure. Then he frowned 'Still, you'd be safer staying at the homestead. There's too many dingo, buffalo, snake and crocodile in this place.'

She held up her hands. 'Stop, please, before you have me heading for the homestead in fright. I've taken plenty of precautions. I have flares, safety equipment and I'm in radio contact with my group.'

Pulling aside the flap of her tent, she revealed a stretcher festooned with gear. In her vehicle was the radio whick kept her in touch with the other members of the Crocodile Task Force in this region. Added to which, her training and field experience protected her, provided she didn't take any stupid chances. Unless she counted leaning out over a crocodile-infested waterway to admire her reflection, she thought ruefully. She hoped Nugget hadn't seen that.

'OK,' he conceded. 'I'll head off. But I'll come back tomorrow to make sure you're all right.'

'Very well.' She knew that he wouldn't be put off by her arguments. As he turned to leave, she noticed his bush horse tethered to a tree in a clearing and she touched his arm. 'You won't tell anyone you've seen me, will you?'

His expression was one of disgust, as if she had no need even to ask. 'My family know you're here. They told me,' he explained. 'The Boss maybe find out but not from me.'

'Thanks. I appreciate it.'

He favoured her with a wide grin which revealed his sparkling white teeth then swung himself on to his horse and was soon swallowed up by the spear grass.

With a feeling of regret, she watched him go. It had been good to talk to him again, after spending the last couple of days on her own. The squawk of the radio was no substitute for face-to-face contact. And Nugget had always been special to her, instilling in her his own love for this wild land.

She let the tent flap fall from her fingers. It was as if Nugget had brought the past with him. She felt it crowding in on her, however much she tried to shut it out.

She had been sixteen when her family came to this area, over three hundred kilometres south-east of Darwin. Her father had been stationed here with the Aerial Medical Service, the former Flying Doctors. Steven Donovan, known as Doctor Donban by the aborigines, had wanted Keri to remain at school in Queensland, near her sister, Louise, but had given in to her pleas to come to the Top End, provided her studies didn't suffer. She had been so anxious for the chance that she studied even harder by correspondence and passed all her exams with flying colours.

Unable to fault her academic performance, her father had taken her with him on his far-flung medical rounds. On one of these trips, she first encountered the Champion family. Jake, the head of the clan, hadn't yet succumbed to the faulty heart valve which eventually claimed his life. Then, he was still King of the Outback, unusually tall in or out of the saddle, and honed to a formidable toughness by his years as a Northern Territory cattle baron.

His daughter, Robyn, had been the reason for Doctor Donovan's visit to the head station, Kinga Downs. Keri's first meeting with Robyn had come as a shock, despite her father's words of preparation during the flight.

'Robyn Champion suffered a brain-stem injury at birth which meant she was born with cerebral palsy. Her muscles don't always do what she wants them to do so her movements are often jerky and uncontrolled. But her brain isn't affected. She's intelligent and full of life. You'll like her.'

His words proved prophetic. Once Keri overcame her initial shock at seeing Robyn's pixie-like form in her special wheelchair, Keri became fascinated by the other girl's use of an alphabet board to communicate.

'Why can't you talk?' she asked with a teenager's typical directness.'

Instead of taking offence, Robyn had appreciated Keri's candour and spelled out laboriously on her board that her throat muscles didn't work well enough to enable her to speak.

'Then how do you manage to eat?' Keri asked

curiously.

'Well enough,' came the spelled response, then the wheelchair rocked with Robyn's laughter as she rubbed her stomach. 'Don't want get fat,' she added on her board.

From then on, the two teenagers became fast friends. Keri flew out with her father at every opportunity and often stayed at Kinga Downs while he completed his rounds. With Keri acting as her voice, Robyn could participate in the School of the Air sessions and they soon became popular members of the scattered class, keeping in touch with the other students by radio.

Robyn's brother, Rick, was an occasional visitor to the lessons. The eldest in the family, he was twenty-two then, and Robyn explained that he was really her half-brother. Rick's natural father had died of a heart attack and his mother had married Jake Champion two years later.

Keri gained the impression that Rick resented not having been born a Champion, unlike Ben, whom she only saw from a distance since he was usually working around the property.

Robyn was the youngest of the three and told Keri through her alphabet board that she had never known her mother. 'She died when you were born?' Keri queried.

Robyn nodded jerkily and stabbed at her board. 'Mum died having me. My fault.'

'No, you mustn't even think it,' Keri insisted. 'Dad told me she died because a flood cut you off from medical help.'

'I was born in a boat,' Robyn's board explained.

'Nearly didn't make it.'

'Well, I'm glad you did,' Keri told her with fierce loyalty. The longer she knew Robyn, the more awed she was by the other girl's courage. The simplest tasks demanded almost superhuman concentration but it didn't stop her from attempting whatever she was able. Her elfin face twisted and she concentrated as if her life depended on it, sweat beading her brow.

Eventually she taught herself to paint with a specially adapted brush and easel. She created outback landscapes of such vibrant beauty that they moved Keri to tears. She sometimes had to remind herself that Robyn was confined to her wheelchair, seeing the landscapes she painted so vividly only from the homestead or through the windows of a Range Rover when one of her brothers took her driving around the property.

It was on one such outing that Keri had her first meeting with Ben Champion. She would never forget that moment.

Jake had left the girls fishing at a billabong along Crocodile Creek while he checked some fences. One minute Keri had been laughing over her clumsy attempts to cast a handline, and the next, she had been staring up at a face drawn from the same gene pool as Clint Eastwood. A thatch of wavy auburn hair strayed across his broad forehead which shaded a gaze that was as penetrating as any searchlight.

He stood with his legs braced apart and his arms loose at his side, the stance creating an impression of tremendous vitality, barely leashed. His taut body quivered with energy like a bowstring before the arrow is released. From Robyn, Keri knew Ben was younger than Rick, but he looked older and wiser with his air of mastery over his environment. Keri had never met anyone who exuded such self-possession. It fascinated and frightened her all at once.

'So you're Robyn's friend,' he said, looking her over as he might have done a new brood mare. 'I'm Ben Champion.'

'I know, I've seen you around the property. I'm Keri Donovan,' she responded, mastering her voice with an effort. Breathing had become difficult suddenly. Desperately she wished for something startlingly original to say but settled for, 'How are you?'

His brown velvet eyes roved over her and she felt their warmth as if he had touched her instead of merely looking. The sensation travelled over her breasts which thrust forward beneath a slightly outgrown T-shirt. Then he made a leisurely tour of her legs outlined in faded denim Levis. It was the most blatant inspection she had ever endured and she felt herself reddening.

'I'm fine, thanks,' he said as those devastating eyes returned to her face at last. 'How come we haven't met before?'

'You were too busy working, I suppose,' she babbled, confused by his attention. He managed to make her feel as if she was the only woman alive. She tried switching her gaze to his mouth instead of those disturbing eyes, but found no respite there either. His strong slanting jaw and wide mouth was saved from arrogance by a full, sensuous lower lip. Quickly, she looked away towards the river.

He chuckled softly, making her jerk her head back
in surprise to find him still watching her with that
infuriating, all-knowing look. 'I'll try not to be so
busy from now on,' he said. Then he thrust his
battered Akubra hat on to his head, swung himself
on to his work horse and cantered away, leaving her
staring after him, mouth agape.

She felt a tug at her T-shirt and looked down.
Robyn was watching her, an expression of glee on
her face. 'What are you laughing at?' she
demanded.

Robyn reached for her alphabet board and spelled
out, 'You two—too much,' then collapsed into
helpless giggles.

True to his word, Ben had spent much more time
at the Kinga Downs homestead from then on. He
was usually busy mending saddles, tinkering with a
motor-bike or breaking a newly caught brumby, but
his eyes inevitably found Keri and lingered there
until she felt his gaze and looked back at him. He
was never too busy to stop and chat with her.

'Are you in love with Ben?' Robyn spelled out one
day on her alphabet board.

Keri shot her a startled glance. 'No! What makes
you ask?'

'You're the first,' Robyn responded, her fingers
busy on the board.

'The first girl he's taken an interest in?' Keri
queried. When Robyn nodded, she shook her head.
'I don't believe it. He thinks of me as another sister,
that's all.'

'You'll see,' came Robyn's cryptic response.

Ben's interest in her, if that was what it was, had

an unexpected side-effect. After barely noticing her existence for two years, Rick Champion began to pay her more attention. The two men were a study in contrasts. Where Ben was serious and hard-working, Rick was fun-loving and adventurous. He was always ready to leave his chores and take the two girls swimming or drive them into town to shop.

He couldn't compare with Ben in looks, Keri acknowledged, but then few men could do that. But Rick was fun to be with and she found herself spending more and more time with him.

When she was with Rick, Keri noticed that Ben became moody and withdrawn. The discovery bothered her for some reason. But he never said anything, and she found herself agreeing with Rick's assessment that Ben objected to them enjoying themselves. Still, it disturbed her that Ben no longer looked at her in a special way and seemed to have taken a dislike to her. It hurt because she wanted to be his friend. 'I don't understand Ben at all,' she confessed to Robyn one day.

'Funny. He says the same about you,' Robyn spelled back.

'Oh, does he?' If he spoke about her to Robyn, he couldn't dislike her so much, could he? 'What else does he say about me?' she asked.

'Not much. Rick says plenty,' Robyn explained through her board. 'He told Ben he would marry you. Ben got mad.'

'Oh, did he?' she repeated thoughtfully, as intrigued by Ben's reaction as by Rick's assurance that they would marry. In the outback, when two people spent as much time together as she and Rick had, marriage usually followed. But was it what she wanted? Granted, Rick was fun to be with and a suitable husband by most social standards, but how did she feel about him as a lifetime partner?

When he finally proposed, she still had no answer ready but told him she would think it over. Unbeknown to her, he had already told Ben that they were engaged. When she sought out Ben to ask his advice, he was coldly uninterested.

'You're old enough to know what you're doing,' he had said before swinging himself into the saddle and riding away. Desolately she had watched him go, feeling as if something important was going out of her life.

For the next few days she didn't see or hear anything from Ben. She wished Rick hadn't told him they were engaged when she felt so uncertain. Rick treated her like a fiancée, feeling free to kiss her when he felt like it. But when she waited for the response she was sure his kiss should provoke, it was curiously absent.

Then had come the dreadful day when Jake Champion was felled by a fatal heart attack and everything changed. Rick disappeared, leaving Ben to take over the running of the properties. He was so busy that Keri didn't have a chance to talk to him until after his father's funeral when they gathered for the reading of Jake's will. Ben sat as far away from her as possible but she was as aware of him as if they had been touching. At that moment she understood why she had avoided giving Rick an answer. Compared to Ben, he paled into insignificance. But how was she to undo the damage she had done by letting him think she had accepted Rick's proposal? She could tell Rick that she had made a mistake, but could she convince Ben that it was really him she cared for?

'Very convenient, isn't it?' he sneered at her when they were finally alone and she could put her feelings into words.

'What do you mean?' she asked, shaken by the derision in his voice. He had never spoken to her like that before.

'Would you have dumped me as readily if Rick had been the one to inherit instead?' he demanded.

'What does that have to do with anything?' she asked, baffled. She had been so busy planning what she would say to Ben that she hadn't heard any of Jake's bequests. She had only attended to help Robyn through the ordeal.

'When you thought Rick was the heir to Champion Holdings, you were happy to marry him. Now you know that he gets nothing except through me, you've decided that your love was misplaced. As I said, very convenient.'

'You're wrong,' she breathed, fighting tears. 'I don't care about the will. I had other things on my mind.'

'Like your future,' he sneered. 'Well, allow me to enlighten you. Although Rick was not Jake's son, he never made any distinction between us. It was only when he began to worry about Rick's free-spending habits that he changed his will to leave Kinga Downs and Casuarina to me. I'm to provide a home and income for Rick but he doesn't inherit any land until he settles down, which leaves his future in my hands.'

'That's not why I can't marry Rick,' she persisted, although the leaden feeling in her stomach told her he didn't believe her. 'I'm not in love with Rick and never was. I was stupid not to tell you before.'

'You're right about one thing,' he observed. 'You were stupid. Stupid to think I'd believe such a tale when the truth is obvious. Rick only has wealth through me, so you want to go where the real money is. I'm disappointed in you, Keri. When you came here I thought you were special. You seemed to care for Robyn and you fitted in here like one of the family. But you're not a Champion and never could be. You don't have the integrity.'

His words had flayed her like a lash, laying open emotional wounds which would take years to heal, if they ever did. If only she had spoken to Ben sooner about her feelings, he might have believed her. Now, she looked like a gold-digger, courting him because Rick had lost his inheritance.

Rick was no kinder to her. He also believed that she was deserting him because he hadn't inherited a fortune. 'A rat deserting a sinking ship,' he called her and worse. When she tried to walk away, he had grabbed her by the shoulders and enveloped her in a cruel travesty of an embrace. What happened next she had buried so deeply in her subconscious that it was still a blur. Her only clear memory was of radioing her father and asking him to collect her on his way back to town. She had vowed never to return to Champion land.

Although it broke her heart to desert Robyn, she

had kept her vow. She told Robyn she was leaving to attend university and gain a degree in environmental science, leading to a career as a ranger with the Conservation Commission. Robyn didn't understand why Keri didn't return even on holidays, but somehow their friendship had survived through letters.

Then Robyn had written with an urgent plea for Keri to come back and help her through the turmoil of Rick's marriage to a neighbouring property heiress, Persia Redshaw. Keri remembered Persia as a frothy, good-natured girl and wondered how Rick could have persuaded her to marry him.

At the same time, Robyn's personal carer of many years' standing had left because of a family crisis and they had not yet been able to replace her. The Champions' housekeeper, Jessie Finch, was happy to look after Robyn, but was finding it a strain on top of running the household. 'I really need you,' Robyn had written, leaving Keri with little choice but to come back.

When the Crocodile Task Force asked her to survey Crocodile Creek which divided the two properties, it seemed like the ideal solution. She wrote to Robyn and told her she would be working close enough to the homestead to enable them to see a good deal of each other.

Gentle probing revealed that Ben spent little time at either homestead, preferring to be out with his men, so there wasn't much chance that Keri would run into him. And with Rick safely married, she managed to quell her apprehension sufficiently to camp on Champion land, where she had never expected to set foot again.

She should have known she would be unable to escape her memories once she was here. Nugget's visit had opened the floodgates.

She was thankful when a disturbance at the edge of the billabong shattered her reverie. Grabbing her camera, she returned to her observation post on the grassy bank. Maybe this time she would get a good photo of one of the giant crocodiles which claimed this billabong as their territory.

There it was. She shuddered involuntarily as a massive scaled head lifted and two clawed forepaws dug into the mud, hauling the creature out of the water like some prehistoric vision. It was huge, at least sixteen feet long she estimated, and she raised her camera.

Before she could take a picture, she was hauled to her feet and thrown backwards. Luckily she landed in thick grass so she was only winded. Her mind functioned at lightning speed, registering the presence of a man with a high-powered rifle levelled at the crocodile.

'Stop, don't shoot it,' she ordered and matched the command with a swift forward motion which pushed the gun aside. With a flick of its tail, the crocodile spun around and slid back into the water. The hunter's breath escaped in a hissing outrush of rage. 'What the hell?'

Her anger was equal to his, but for different reasons 'Don't you know it's illegal to shoot crocodiles in this state?'

'It's legal when someone's life is in danger,' he

snapped back. 'You were within feet of being eaten.'

'I was nothing of the sort. I was doing my job perfectly well until you came along.'

Her head jerked upwards and her eyes met his. Only then did she realise whom she had thwarted, and she went cold from head to foot. He realised her identity at the same moment and they said as one, 'You!'

'Ben Champion, I might have known,' she gasped.

'Keri Donovan, I should have known,' he echoed. 'What were you doing, trying to get yourself killed?'

'I'm conducting a survey for the Crocodile Task Force of the Conservation Commission,' she said haughtily, drawing out each syllable.

If she had hoped to impress him, she was disappointed. His tawny gaze raked the wedge-tailed eagle insignia on her shoulder patch then returned to her face. His expression was chilly. 'You still need the owner's permission to be on this land. I don't recall giving it.'

'Robyn gave it,' she said and saw the flicker of annoyance on his face. 'She is a part-owner of Champion Holdings, isn't she?'

'You know damned well she is. I wouldn't be surprised if you could quote me the par value of her shares. I recall you take more than a passing interest in such matters.'

She clenched and unclenched her fists at her sides. So time hadn't mellowed his attitude towards her. He still thought her only interest was in the Champion money. 'If that's what you think, I can't help it, but the truth is I came here because Robyn asked me to. After losing her old nurse, she needed a friend, especially after the upheaval of Rick getting married.'

His eyes narrowed. 'Don't you mean *when* Rick gets married?'

Apprehension rippled through her. 'Isn't he married yet?'

His lip curled into a sneer. 'No, he isn't. The marriage was to have been held last weekend, but Persia's grandmother had a stroke and Persia flew to Darwin to take care of her. The wedding was postponed for a month.'

Despairingly, she shook her head. 'I didn't know. I thought it would be over by now.'

'I'll bet you did.'

His body was aligned in a posture of contempt for her. The jutting hip and folded arms shut out any defence she could have offered against his accusations. Body language did speak louder than words, and his pose announced what he thought of her in no uncertain terms.

Still, she had to try to make him understand. 'You're wrong,' she said with all the dignity she could muster. 'I've been out in the field for a week. I didn't know the wedding had been postponed, or I wouldn't have come.'

'So you didn't know that I was giving Rick the deeds to Casuarina as a wedding present?'

'I read about it in the newspapers, but it has nothing to do with me.'

'You didn't come here hoping for a second chance with Rick?'

'No!' The protest was wrung from her with such

sincerity that even Ben looked uncertain for a moment. Then his eyes hardened.

'I can't take a chance on trusting you, I'm afraid.'

Was he going to order her off his land? 'You can tell me to leave and I'll go, but Robyn is the one you'll be hurting,' she said. 'She's already looking forward to our reunion.'

'You're despicable,' he ground out. 'To think you would use someone in Robyn's situation to get your own way. What you did to Rick was bad enough, but this is too much.'

She let his words rain around her, trying not to let them penetrate the armour she had built around herself since she left Kinga Downs. Then she had vowed never to let Ben get close enough to hurt her again. Already it was proving to be much harder than she had anticipated.

While she still had some defences left, she turned away from him, meaning to pack her things and leave. But as she started up the slope, he swung her around, his hard fingers biting into the tender flesh of her upper arm. 'Where are you going?'

'Anywhere as long as it's away from here,' she said, not looking at him.

He cupped her chin in one hand and brought her head up until their eyes met. 'Running away again?' he taunted.

She shrugged. 'You don't give me much choice.'

The sensuously curving mouth she had once imagined on hers tautened into an implacable line. 'You haven't heard me out yet.'

Hope flared briefly inside her then was crushed as she caught sight of the diamond-bright glint in his eyes. Whatever choice she was to be offered, she didn't think she would like it.

'You're right about Robyn needing you,' he said shortly. 'I know how unhappy she's been since her carer left. It wouldn't be good for her if I sent you away, now she knows that you're coming.'

'So what are you going to do?'

'I'm going to make sure you don't cause trouble between Rick and Persia, while you keep your promise to Robyn.'

Some of her own spirit flared and she jerked her arm free, rubbing it so that he would see that he had bruised her. 'How do you propose to do that—keep me on a leash by your side?'

His mouth twitched. 'In a way. The leash I have in mind is an engagement ring.'

CHAPTER TWO

UNABLE to believe her ears, she stared at him. 'I don't want to be engaged to you.'

'I didn't say you had to want it. You just have to do it.'

'But why? What good will it do?'

Ben braced his back against a tree trunk and rested his rifle beside him. 'If Rick thinks you're my property, he'll keep his eyes on Persia where they belong. You can't be so naïve that you haven't heard about his exploits while you've been counting crocodiles?'

'I've heard.' She didn't add that for months after she left Kinga Downs she had devoured every scrap of published information about the Champion family. Most of the stories had been about Rick, who seemed to be working his way through the social register and a good slice of the family fortune, judging by the lavish parties and chartered air tours she read about.

When Ben was mentioned it was usually in a business connection. Once or twice she had seen his name linked with some local beauty, but mostly it appeared that he devoted his time to running Champion Holdings.

When she didn't elaborate, Ben went on. 'Then you know he hasn't exactly settled down since Dad died. Persia Redshaw is the first woman he's taken a serious interest in, and I don't want anything to interfere with this marriage.'

'I know you don't believe me, but I didn't come back to interfere. Before I left, I told you how I felt about Rick, and my feelings haven't changed.'

'None of your feelings?' he asked tensely.

Stealing a glance at him, she was astonished to find him regarding her almost warmly. She must be imagining it, she told herself. His dislike of her was as strong as ever, judging by the preposterous condition he was setting on her staying here.

'None of my feelings,' she said firmly and let him make of it what he would. Once before, she had made the mistake of baring her soul to him and he had flung it in her face. She wasn't about to give him such a chance again.

All the same, she was disturbingly aware of how her nerve-endings quivered in response to his presence. She told herself it was only tension but her body persisted in bending towards him like a sapling in the wind.

'In that case my proposition should solve the problem,' he continued.

'No, it's ridiculous. I don't know why I'm even discussing it with you.'

'Maybe you find some attraction in the idea,' he suggested. 'I could make it worth your while.'

He thought she was angling for payment for her co-operation, she realised, and the idea drenched her like a cold shower. About to contradict him, she stopped. If she let him think so, it would be easier to keep her distance while was was with Robyn. 'Who would believe we had decided to get married out of the blue?' she asked with apparent wariness.

'It wouldn't have to be out of the blue if I had been courting you secretly,' he pointed out. 'I spend a lot of time in Darwin on business. I could have been seeing you at the same time.'

She tugged a hand through her hair, spilling curls around her face in a protective curtain. 'But you weren't, were you?'

Unexpectedly, he reached out and touched the shining curls with the back of one finger. 'How do you know I wasn't? I know you've been catching crocodiles in Darwin Harbour and dating that Greek millionaire.'

Her eyes met his, dark with confusion. Could he have been watching her? The idea set her pulses racing until common sense reasserted itself. 'You read those things in Darwin newspapers, didn't you?' Seeing her name in print had shaken her at the time, but she had told herself it would soon be forgotten. Apparently not by Ben.

He nodded. 'As it happens, I did. But it does provide a sound background for our courtship, so an engagement won't come as a complete surprise.'

'Except to Robyn,' she reminded him. 'She'll wonder why I haven't mentioned seeing you in my letters.'

'Then she'll have to wonder,' he said smoothly. 'Even best friends are entitled to their secrets.'

To her amazement, she found she was actually considering his proposition. Just in time she remembered why he was so insistent. 'The answer is still no,' she said, recovering some of her composure. 'If I'm to stay, you'll have to take my word that I won't came between Rick and Persia.'

Instantly he was businesslike again. 'I've seen what your word is worth, remember? I can't take the chance. But since you won't agree to my condition for seeing Robyn, you can plan on visiting her in hospital.'

She lifted shocked eyes to him. 'What?'

'Her doctor says if she doesn't recover her strength soon, she'll need a spell in hospital so they can build her up.'

'You bastard,' she seethed. 'You know I'd never let that happen if I could prevent it.'

He was indifferent to her anger. 'Suit yourself,' he said coolly.

'You've made sure that I can't suit myself,' she retorted. 'I'll have to play it your way or Robyn will be the one to suffer.'

'Then you agree?'

'I agree.' Her capitulation came out sullenly, but she was also conscious of a spark of energy inside her which hadn't been there moments before. It was as if his challenge had ignited a fuse within her. She tried to quiet the tremulous feelings by reminding herself that he only wanted to keep her on his idea of a leash so that she wouldn't spoil Rick's chance at a settled life with Persia Redshaw.

Ben's next words confirmed it. 'Naturally, you'll come and stay at Kinga Downs.'

Her eyelashes flicked back, exposing her wide-eyed gaze to him. 'I didn't agree to move in with you.'

'But you will, for Robyn's sake. She'll think it strange if you don't stay at the homestead with us.'

'Where you can keep an eye on me,' she finished his thought. When he didn't contradict her, she added, 'What about my work?

'You can drive back here as often as necessary, or one of my men can bring you.'

'That's big of you,' she said sarcastically. 'How long is this charade supposed to go on?'

He met her challenging look impassively. 'A month ought to be enough to see Rick safely married.'

'A month? In that case I'd better arrange to take some leave so that I can give you my undivided attention,' she said in a tone which dripped sarcasm.

Instead of the anger she had intended to provoke, he reacted with enthusiasm. 'An excellent suggestion. If you get bored, you can always continue your survey here. I'm sure the Conservation Commission won't mind if you offer to work during your leave.'

'They might as well join the bandwagon and have my services for free,' she rejoined.

His brows drew together ominously. 'I haven't asked you to do anything for free. I'm well aware of the high price you put on yourself.'

She gave a theatrical sigh. 'When will you believe that I'm not after the Champion fortune? I wasn't before and I'm not this time.'

He patted his hands together in soundless applause. 'Keep it up and I'll end up believing you.'

No, he wouldn't, she thought miserably. He saw only what he wanted to see. He would be astonished if he knew that Rick couldn't marry Persia Redshaw fast enough for Keri's liking.

While Ben stood by, she contacted the leader of her group and arranged to take some leave. She had several weeks owing to her, and her boss sounded pleased when he heard that she finally wanted some time off. At Ben's insistence, she allowed him to speak to her boss. When he thumbed the receiver off, he looked satisfied. 'It's all set,' he informed her. 'They're happy for you to continue the survey in your own time, but I'm instructed not to let you work too hard. Your boss has quite a high opinion of you.'

'Which is more than some people have,' she retorted. When he didn't respond she set about breaking camp, packing up her supplies and equipment in thoughtful silence. She was aware of Ben working alongside her and every time their bodies touched in passing, she felt a jolt like an electric current arc along her veins. Fighting the response, she reminded herself that she was doing this for Robyn's sake, not to revive a teenage infatuation with Ben which had already hurt her enough for a lifetime.

'Is that the lot?'

She marshalled her whirling thoughts. 'Yes, that's everything.'

'Then let's go.' He climbed into the driver's seat of her Conservation Commission vehicle.

'What about your car?'

'I'll send one of the men for it later.'

Rather than endure a trip to Kinga Downs at his side, she debated whether to insist that they drove both cars in convoy. But the sooner she satisfied herself that she was Ben-proof, the better. Without an argument, she climbed into the passenger seat.

The four-wheel-drive vehicle was soon jolting along the rutted road to Kinga Downs homestead. In an attempt to avoid thinking too much about the man beside her, she concentrated on the jungle-like terrain which covered most of the Champion properties. Altogether they encompassed well over a million acres of land. Kinga Downs was two thousand square miles in area and Casuarina was smaller but still sizeable at five hundred square miles.

Crocodile Creek, an offshoot of the vast South Alligator River system, divided the two properties and watered the grazing lands on which roved the shorthorns and polls of the Champion cattle herds. The rest of the land was the province of the buffalo, brumby, dingo and crocodile and the remnants of the Myall aborigines whose traditional homeland adjoined the Champion empire. To the stockmen, this was Dreamtime Country and the Myalls were the Stone Men of myth and legend.

She shifted her gaze sideways. Ben was a stone man, but of a different kind, flint-hard and unreachable. She let her eyes rest on his hands which were work-roughened and tanned to a deep mahogany and thought of his feather-light touch against her hair. It must have been a momentary lapse. She couldn't believe that those hands could be soft and caressing. 'Why were you going to shoot that crocodile?' she asked suddenly, not caring to think too far along those lines.

'I was only going to scare it away from you,' he explained. 'It's been taking cattle along that stretch of the river. When I saw it coming close to you, I didn't want you becoming the next victim.'

'You're sure it's the same animal?' she queried.

He glanced at her then back to the road. 'Don't you think so?'

'There are two big crocs in that waterhole—a male and a female. I've seen the male once from a distance and he has a deformed jaw, which would explain why he's taking cattle. The one I was photographing today is a female. I think she's nesting along that stretch of bank, although I haven't found a nest yet.'

'If you're right, the female will only be aggressive until her young hatch. But the injured male ought to be shifted to new territory before somebody gets hurt.'

'Moving him won't help,' she explained. 'The instinct to home in on one particular pool will bring him right back here in time. Only recently, we had a crocodile which travelled overland more than forty miles to get back to its old territory.'

The warmth in her voice caught his attention. 'You really enjoy your job, don't you? You even care for these prehistoric monsters.'

'I suppose I do,' she admitted. 'Ever since Nugget taught me to love the wild and all its creatures, I've wanted to make it my career. I was lucky that it worked out so well.'

The vehicle took flight over a series of bumps and Ben wrestled it back under control again then asked, 'What would you have done if you couldn't become a ranger?'

She was tempted to jest that she would have

married a rich grazier, but since that was already what he expected from her, she decided not to joke about it. 'Probably joined the Aerial Medical Service like Mum and Dad, if I could hack it.'

'How are your parents?' he asked her.

'They're fine. They live in North Queensland now so they can be close to Louise.'

He took his eyes off the road momentarily. 'She's your sister, I remember. Isn't she autistic?'

'Yes. She attends a special boarding school in Queensland. Soon she'll be getting a job in a sheltered workshop. Then she'll move into a group home where she'll learn to live as normal a life as possible.'

He slipped the car into four-wheel drive as they approached a shallow creek-crossing. At the end of the dry season, there was little water to soften the corrugated mud bottom as they jolted across it. 'I suppose that's why you're so good with Robyn, because of your sister,' he guessed.

'I'm good with Robyn because she's a terrific person,' she said irritably. 'Look, I know you think I'm a gold-digger, but Robyn is my friend, not some good cause I've taken on.'

'If I thought otherwise, I wouldn't let you within coo-ee of her,' he said grimly, man-handling the vehicle up the steep bank of the creek. 'I realise you do have *some* redeeming qualities.'

'Let's be thankful for small mercies,' she muttered under her breath, then turned her head away and pretended rapt interest in the scenery.

They didn't speak again until they reached the cluster of buildings which made up Kinga Downs

homestead. More like a small town than a single
dwelling, it was home to the station manager,
jackeroos, carpenters, plumber, stockmen and book-
keepers who helped to run Champion Holdings.

In the centre of the cluster was the main
homestead, a handsome turn-of-the-century timber
structure screened with lattice panels which ensured
privacy while admitting every scrap of breeze. The
verandas which surrounded the house were floored
with spotted gum weathered to an attractive silver-
grey, in contrast to the cool green paint on the walls.
Behind the house, was a pool area paved with ochre-
coloured stones which echoed the colour of the
Champion land itself.

There were no steps leading to the main house,
only ramps which provided access for Robyn's
wheelchair. Now, Keri saw that similar access had
been provided to nearly all the buildings around the
homestead.

As soon as they pulled up in the shade of a giant
Poinsettia tree, a flyscreen door flew open and
Robyn appeared in her wheelchair, her face alight
with excitement. Keri dropped her things and ran to
her friend, crouching down to give her a warm hug.
'It's so good to see you again,' she whispered in
Robyn's ear. In truth, she was shocked at how thin
Robyn had become. Her wrists and ankles were
mostly bone and her sparkling eyes looked huge in
her pale face.

Keri was careful not to let her distress show. The
last thing Robyn ever wanted was pity. She made
her smile broader. 'Let's go inside. Ben says he'll
get someone to take care of my luggage.'

At the mention of luggage, Robyn's head bobbed up and down vigorously and she tugged questioningly at Keri's shirt sleeve.

'Yes, Ben talked me into staying here,' she said in answer to Robyn's unspoken question. She decided to let Ben break the rest of their news to his sister. She had never lied to Robyn before and she didn't know how to start now.

Inside, the double drawing-room was cool and welcoming. A pair of kumquat trees in heavy cane baskets flanked a window and potted plants were in abundance. Sofas and chairs slip-covered in floral linen made conversational groups around the huge room and an old drum acted as a drinks table. On a tripod table, Robyn's collection of Georgian and Victorian silver gleamed from its owner's frequent polishing.

Keri made a small pirouette in the centre of the room. 'This room is still as beautiful as ever,' she exclaimed.

Robyn wheeled herself over to a window. Beneath it was a side table on which sat a computer complete with screen and printer. It looked startlingly modern alongside the antique silverware. 'Is this yours?' Keri asked, bending over it.

Close-up, she saw that the keyboard had been modified to accommodate Robyn's exaggerated movements. The woman settled herself in front of it and with a few keystrokes brought the screen to life. 'My new alphabet board,' she typed and the words flashed on to the screen.

'How marvellous! It's so much faster,' Keri enthused.

'That's not all,' came the typed response. 'Look.'

Before Keri's astonished eyes, Robyn worked a separate keypad and made lights flash on and off around the room. At another touch, shutters lowered over the windows then lifted again, and a wooden-bladed fan began to whir overhead.

Keri hugged her friend. 'I'm impressed.'

'Computer in the kitchen works appliances,' Robyn typed on her screen. 'Keypad in my room works bedroom and bathroom.'

Ben had done his sister proud, Keri thought with a choked feeling. No expense had been spared to ensure that she could enjoy as independent a life as possible. But there was another surprise in store for her.

'Robyn achieved most of this by herself.'

Keri straightened to find Ben lounging in the doorway, watching them. He saw the surprise flicker across her face. 'You remember those outback paintings she used to do?'

She nodded. 'They were excellent.'

'Quite a few people agree, enough to provide Rob with a good income.'

The insistent tapping of the keyboard drew Keri's attention. 'Most buyers don't know the painter is handicapped,' Robyn typed.

Keri dropped to her knees beside the wheelchair and gripped her friend's arm. 'That's because they think like me. How can you be handicapped when you give the world so much?'

Tears glistened in Robyn's eyes and she enveloped Keri's hands in both of hers. The wordless welcome couldn't have been plainer.

Ben came into the room and placed both hands on his sister's shoulders. 'There's more good news to come. Have you told her yet?'

Robyn's questioning glance flew to Keri and she shook her head. 'I was waiting for you.'

'How thoughtful of you,' he said drily. 'Well, we mustn't keep Rob in suspense. Keri has agreed to become my wife.'

With an indrawn gasp, Robyn swivelled to her keyboard and typed in capital letters, 'Yippee!!' with a string of exclamation points which went off the edge of the screen. Then she wrapped her arms around Keri in a hug which drove the breath out of her.

Ben's eyebrows arched upwards. 'Somehow, I think she likes the idea.'

Releasing Keri, Robyn typed on her keyboard. 'How? When? Where?'

'Steady on, all in good time,' Ben said good-humouredly, and dropped into a chair so that he was at his sister's level. Then he told her the story he had concocted, about seeing Keri in Darwin on his business trips there.

'You dark horses,' Robyn typed, adding, 'but I'm thrilled.'

Which made one of them, Keri thought darkly as she excused herself to go to her room and unpack. Robyn's reaction had made her feel ten times as bad about the deception. It was all very well for Ben to dream up a fake engagement to keep Rick's eyes from wandering, but Robyn would be hurt when she found out the truth. Couldn't Ben see the damage his scheme could do to his sister?

Despairingly, she looked around the bedroom, but there was no solace there. Ben had given her the white bedroom, a romantic confection of lace-edged pillows and embroidered cotton and lace swathing the bed. A cane sofa was massed with white-embossed cotton cushions. Curtains in the same material added to the romantic effect. It was the sort of room a bride-to-be would feel at home in, and it made Keri feel even more of a fraud. She thrust her few clothes into the nearest drawers and went out on to the veranda through a door opening off her room.

Gripping the hardwood railing, she stared unseeingly at the garden which separated the main house from the other buildings. She knew that Ben had joined her when her senses began to quiver, and she turned to him, her eyes dark with concern. 'I can't go through with it, Ben. Can't you see?'

He looked troubled, too, but shook his head. 'It's too late to back out now. Rob is already planning our engagement party.'

'Oh, no. That makes me feel even worse.'

He hooked a boot over the bottom rail of the veranda and propped his elbows on the top one. 'If it's any consolation, I feel just as bad. I should have known that Rob would go overboard once she heard the news. She's always thought of you as a sister, so this merely confirms your role.'

'I suppose we should be glad that it's doing her so much good,' she said dourly.

He sighed. 'It's an ill wind . . .'

She turned to face him, her temper flaring. 'That's all very well, but what about when the truth comes out? How will she feel then, knowing we lied to her?'

'The truth doesn't have to come out,' he said stonily.

'What do you mean?'

'I mean we could make it a real engagement.' He turned towards the garden, seemingly thinking aloud. 'I need a wife. There should be an heir to all this. You love this country and your work is here. It could suit us both very well.'

'You make it sound so businesslike,' she observed, adding the question which was uppermost in her mind but not, it seemed, in his. 'What about love?'

At her softly voiced question, he turned the full force of his velvety gaze on her, caressing her with his look until her heart began to hammer in her chest. 'There could be love,' he said. 'I could love you as you've never been loved before.'

As she realised what kind of love he meant, she shuddered. 'I didn't mean sexual love. The kind of love I meant starts with caring, sharing and respect.'

His expression became cold. 'I'm afraid they have to be earned.'

She opened her mouth to argue but a cloud of dust along the driveway announced the arrival of another car. It screeched to a halt outside the main homestead and a man got out. Her spirits sank even lower as the man approached them. 'G'day, little brother. You should have told me we were expecting company.'

He moved closer and Keri became aware of tension radiating from Ben's lithe body. 'She isn't here to see you, Rick,' he said coldly. 'Keri is my guest.'

'Keri? My God, is that really you? You've blossomed into a beauty. How about a kiss for Rick?'

As her stomach muscles clenched in protest at the very idea, Ben stepped between them. 'I said she's here as *my* guest.' He emphasised the possessive pronoun.

Rick spread his hands apart. 'OK, I get the message. Hands off.' For now, his tone suggested. She shivered. Then feeling that she must say something, she volunteered, 'Hello, Rick.'

'Hello yourself. Since when did the skinny teenager turn into such a beauty, and in a ranger's uniform yet? I'll bet you look fantastic in a bikini.'

'It's not something you're likely to find out,' Ben ground out.

Rick's temper, which Keri remembered only too vividly, got the better of him. 'Now hang on, little brother. How about letting the lady speak for herself?'

Ben took a menacing step towards Rick. 'Call me little brother again and I'll flatten you.'

'Why? She's not your property, is she?'

'As it happens, she is. Keri and I are engaged to be married.'

Rick looked as if he had been felled by a blow. His face crumpled and he balled his hands into fists at his sides. 'This is pretty sudden, isn't it?'

'We've been seeing each other in Darwin,' Ben said, the smooth lie sounding more and more polished to Keri's outraged ears.

'Stop it, you two,' she said, stepping between

them. 'As it happens, I'm nobody's property.'

'I see you've lost none of your spirit,' Rick said in a tone of grudging admiration. 'It's going to be fun having you back.'

'Aren't you forgetting something?' Ben interrupted.

Rick dragged his eyes away from Keri. 'Like what?'

'Like a fiancée of your own?'

Rick looked as if he would like to hit Ben, but was forced to nod agreement. Then he winked and added, 'But while the cat's away . . .'

Which was exactly the situation Ben had feared when he found out that she was back. 'There'll be no playing,' she said coldly. How could he even think she would be interested after what had happened last time? Already, his nearness was making her flesh crawl. 'You heard Ben. I'm going to marry him.'

How plausible it sounded when she said it with such conviction. Rick looked taken aback. Then his unshakeable self-confidence reasserted itself. 'A lot can happen between an engagement and a marriage,' he said, fixing her with an exaggerated wink. Before Ben could react, he grabbed her hand and lifted it close to his face. 'I don't even have to compete with a ring yet.'

She paled as she realised that Ben had overlooked the most obvious symbol of their status. 'We haven't had time to choose one yet,' she dissembled, throwing Ben a look of appeal.

He moved to her side and Rick stepped back just as quickly. 'No need to get excited, Ben. I was just commenting on an obvious lack. I'm sure you plan to remedy it soon.'

He isn't fooled, she thought with a sinking heart. More than ever, she wished she hadn't agreed to come to the homestead, far less to this travesty of an engagement which only seemed to be fooling Robyn, the last person she wanted to cheat.

'I'm saving the ring to give to Keri at Robyn's party,' Ben supplied.

Rick's eyes narrowed and his expression remained sceptical. 'This I have to see,' he muttered as he stormed off the veranda. Over his shoulder, he added, 'At your buck's night, remind me to tell you a few things about your bride-to-be.'

'You can't tell me anything I don't know,' Ben insisted.

'Then you already know about the heart-shaped birthmark around her left nipple,' Rick said as he walked away.

Anger and disgust warred with one another on Ben's face as he confronted Keri. 'Don't tell me that you and Rick . . .'

'No, no,' she cut across him before he could accuse her and Rick of being lovers.

'Then he was bluffing about the birthmark?'

When she remained silent, shivering with tension, he reached forward and unhooked the top two buttons of her shirt.

CHAPTER THREE

SHE stood mesmerised, unable to move a muscle as Ben's fingers connected with the sensitive skin of her throat. One by one, he flicked the buttons of her shirt aside, revealing the deep cleft between her breasts. As he reached for the next button, she came to her senses and knocked his hand away. 'Stop that.'

His hand froze in mid-gesture and he searched her face. 'Then it's true, you and Rick were lovers.'

'It isn't any of your business, but we weren't,' she denied, finding that she didn't want him to think so even for a minute.

'But you were engaged to him?'

'Not officially. I hadn't made up my mind.'

His lip curled into a sneer. 'You made it up quickly enough once you found out what was in Dad's will. You were only too keen to dump Rick once you knew how things stood.'

Her sigh of frustration exploded on the air between them. 'It's useless trying to make you understand. I suppose you never did anything stupid in your life?'

'Oh, but I did. It haunts me still and there isn't a thing I can do to take it back.'

His quiet admission stunned her. He was so arrogant, so sure of himself, that she couldn't imagine him doing anything foolish, far less letting himself be haunted by it. 'Then you should be able to make allowances for other people,' she flung at him.

'I thought that's what I was doing.'

'If that's the point of this fake engagement, it isn't going to work. Rick has already seen through it, I'm certain.'

'Maybe you didn't try hard enough to convince him,' he observed.

Impatiently, she tossed her head, spilling golden curls around her shoulders. 'Just how do you suggest I convince him?' she demanded.

She knew she had said the wrong thing when he moved closer and she glimpsed the determined gleam in his eyes. 'What are you doing?'

'Helping you to be more convincing,' he said and closed the small remaining gap.

The strength of his embrace drove the breath out of her body, silencing any protest she might have made. In spite of her resolve, a frisson of pleasure rippled through her as his hard contours moulded against her soft ones. Against all common sense, she found herself yielding.

When he kissed her, her lips were already parted in anticipation. The taste and scent of his outdoorsy masculinity flooded her senses, as heady as wine.

After what seemed like an eternity he lifted his head. He was also breathing fast and his eyes were stormy. She tried to tell herself he was playing a role, but that didn't explain why he looked every bit as shaken as she felt.

'Keep this up and you'll have me believing you love me,' he said, his husky tone at odds with the taunting words.

She blinked hard, fighting his spell. It was as if her old feelings had been covered by a thin veil which his kiss had torn aside. Now it was a struggle to put it back into place. 'No, I won't, because I can't go on with this.' How could she when every instinct urged her to get away from him before he destroyed the veil entirely?

He caught her as she turned away. 'What are you going to do?'

'What I should have done from the first, be honest with Robyn. She deserves at least that much from me.'

'You can't do it.' The harsh denial sounded as if it had been wrung from him.

She tugged her arm free. 'Yes, I can. I was crazy to go along with the idea even for a short time.'

'You knew it would be good for Robyn.'

'But it isn't quite that noble, remember? Your only interest is in keeping me from interfering in this highly suitable marriage you've lined up for Rick.'

'The marriage was Rick's own idea,' Ben said tiredly. 'It's the first decent thing he's done in years and I don't want anyone spoiling it for him.'

Especially not her, Keri added silently. 'You needn't worry on my account,' she assured him. 'I'll have my talk with Robyn then leave quietly. You won't need a fake engagement to keep me in line if I'm not here to cause trouble.'

His eyes flashed fire. 'So you admit that's what you came here for?'

She sighed. 'If you say so. Do you mind letting me go so I can talk to Robyn?'

He released her and his fingers traced a line down her arm, lingering on the pliant skin of her wrist. He must feel the insistent throbbing which her pulse suddenly set up, she thought, but he dropped his hand. 'What are you waiting for?' he demanded when she hesitated.

She fled into the house. When she looked back he was striding across the garden towards the stockmen's quarters. Briefly she wondered what stupid thing he had ever done. She would give a lot to know.

She located Robyn in the kitchen, working her computer console to search through her recipe files. Helping her was Jessie Finch, the Champions' cook-housekeeper who now doubled as Robyn's personal carer. A plump, middle-aged woman, she had a china-doll complexion and lilac-tinted grey hair. She was also one of the nicest people Keri had ever met.

Coming between them, Keri put one arm around Robyn's thin shoulders and the other around Jessie's waist. 'What are you two plotting? Tonight's dinner?'

Jessie shook her head. 'We plan the meals a week in advance these days. Robyn was hunting out recipes for the party, weren't you, dear?'

Robyn's head bobbed enthusiastically. She cleared the screen with the press of a key then typed in. 'Everybody's invited. Can't wait.'

Something sharp and painful twisted in Keri's stomach. Robyn's expectant face was alight with a pleasure which hadn't been there when Keri arrived. 'I wanted to talk to you about the party,' she said diffidently.

'I know, no fuss,' Robyn typed out. 'I forgot you hate crowds.' She cocked her head and waited, eyeing Keri anxiously.

'We can keep the numbers down, if that's what's bothering you,' Jessie supplied.

It wasn't but she decided to let them think so. Robyn was too frail to cope with the truth, as well Ben knew when he allowed her to escape so easily. 'Yes, that's it,' she said on a deep sigh.

Some of the tension flowed out of Robyn's fragile body. She returned to her keyboard and typed, 'OK. We invite half the district, not all of it.'

Jessie patted Robyn's shoulder. 'That's the idea. Now is there anything special you'd like on the menu?' she asked Keri.

'Whatever you two decide is fine with me,' she demurred. On the pretext of not wanting to interrupt their work, she escaped from the kitchen and returned to her bedroom.

What had she got herself into? Ben knew how Robyn would react when he concocted this ridiculous engagement. No doubt he was counting on it to ensure Keri's continued compliance. She began to wish she had agreed to leave the Champion property altogether.

Why hadn't she simply left when she had the chance? It couldn't be because she wanted to see Ben again, despite everything—could it?

She already knew that he wasn't going to change his mind about her. His actions today proved it. So why did he want her to stay here?

Needing the distraction of work, she rummaged in her luggage and took out her notebook. Soon she

was immersed in recording her latest sighting of the
female crocodile at Crocodile Creek. It was late in
the afternoon by the time she finished and she
decided to take a walk around the homestead. She
was curious to see what changes Ben had made to
the place since he succeeded Jake as head of the
Champion empire.

Most of the changes were subtle. Some new
buildings had gone up, all with access ramps for
Robyn's wheelchair. There was a new power-plant
fuelled by the wind generators Ben had shown her as
they drove in. He had also pointed out a new all-
weather airstrip which connected the properties with
the outside world during the wet season when many
roads became impassable.

The most noticeable change was in the behaviour
of the men. Whatever they were doing— tinkering
with motor-bikes, branding calves or tilling the
homestead vegetable garden—they did with an air of
pride and purpose. It was the way Ben did
everything, she thought. He inspired his men to do
the same.

At the breaking yards, she came up short, awed
by the sight of a magnificent, fearless horseman
astride a wild brumby which threshed and lashed
defiantly, resisting the rider's attempt to tame it.
Inch by inch, the breaker imposed his will until the
horse's arched-back leaps became less spectacular,
finally stopping altogether. Head down, flanks
heaving, it stood still while the horseman patted its
neck to reassure it.

As if he felt her scrutiny, the rider looked up and
their eyes met. Keri's breath caught in her throat.

She hadn't recognised Ben under the battered bushman's hat, although she should have known his style. She dropped her gaze first and fancied she heard his mocking chuckle as she walked on.

It was pure fantasy, but she felt a sudden surge of empathy with the wild horse he had ridden into submission. Her breathing quickened in sympathy and she felt chokingly hot, as if the dust of the breaking-yard had penetrated her nostrils. She shook her head to throw off the image. If Ben had any notion of breaking her as he had just done the brumby, he was in for the fight of his life.

'If looks could kill, he's a dead man,' said a voice behind her.

She swung around to find Rick jogging to catch up with her. 'Who is?' she asked, feeling her tension grow as he approached.

'Big Ben,' he said. 'I saw you watching him just now. It was him you were thinking of, wasn't it?'

'No, it wasn't,' she denied, unwilling to agree with Rick about anything and especially not about Ben. 'I could have been thinking about you.'

He rolled his eyes expressively. 'I should be so lucky.'

'Did you want something?' she asked, tiring of the game.

He draped an arm around a fence post and appraised her thoughtfully. 'You know what I want. What I've always wanted from you.'

'Stop it,' she ordered, shaken in spite of herself. 'You're engaged. If Persia's grandmother hadn't been taken ill, you'd be married by now.'

'Married isn't dead,' he informed her. 'I intend to

go through with the wedding all right. How else can I get my hands on Casuarina?'

'Surely that isn't the only reason you're marrying Persia?'

He shrugged. 'It's as good a reason as any. It will be worth it if it persuades Ben to sign the outstation over to me. It's what our father wanted. Ben told me.'

'Why are you telling me this?' she asked uncomfortably. 'I could go straight to Ben.'

'But you won't because of what I'd do in return,' he said nastily. 'My parting shot about the birthmark got to Ben, didn't it? I could tell him much more.'

'Why are you doing this?' she asked. 'You've got what you want.'

'Not quite. Title to Casuarina is the most important thing, of course, but Persia won't satisfy me for long.' She started to move away but he caught her wrist. 'Don't rush away. I haven't had a chance to tell you my proposition yet.'

Held fast, she averted her gaze. 'I'm not interested. I'm engaged to Ben and you're going to marry Persia, so there's nothing for us to discuss.'

'I wasn't proposing marriage,' he contradicted. 'When I'm in control of Casuarina, I'll be able to give you everything you want. It won't be like last time, when you went away because I couldn't take care of you. This time it'll be better. You don't have to settle for second best.'

'Second best? You can't mean Ben?' she asked, her tone incredulous.

He nodded. 'You only turned to him because I

was cut out of Jake's will. It's all right,' he added when she jerked away in protest at his monstrous assumption, 'I'd have done the same. But there's no need this time. I can give you everything your heart desires.'

The glare she gave him would have melted a block of ice. 'The only thing I desire from you is to be left alone,' she said, forcing the words between clenched jaws. 'Now let me go.'

Still he refused to give up. 'You were mine before Ben had any claim on you.'

Her head swung back. 'Not in the way you mean.'

'Ben doesn't know that,' he reminded her.

'You made sure he would think so, didn't you?' she said angrily.

'So he was interested in how I knew about the birthmark,' he speculated. 'He must feel something for you after all.'

She kept her gaze haughtily averted. 'It's really none of your business.'

He swung her around so she was forced to look at him. 'I wouldn't use that high and mighty tone if I were you. You weren't too proud to go out with me when you thought I had money. Well, I will have again, but on my own terms this time, not on brother Ben's sufferance. You'll change your tune then.' He lowered his head and spoke close to her ear. 'You see, I know what Ben's up to.'

'Why does he have to be up to anything?' She managed to speak normally but her voice trembled with the effort.

'Because I know him. This romance of yours is too sudden to be true. He's up to his old trick of coming between me and anything I want, but he isn't getting away with it this time.'

'Don't I have something to say in this?' she asked, trying to keep her tone light.

He traced a finger along her jawline and she flinched in spite of herself. At her involuntary gesture, his frown deepened. 'I know you want me, Keri. Your protests are for Ben's benefit, but once I'm master of Casuarina you won't have to fear him. I'll be able to protect you. It'll be good, you'll see.'

His colossal conceit and his total misunderstanding of the situation almost robbed her of the power of speech. She found her voice with an effort. 'You're wrong. I'm not scared of Ben. I'm going to marry him.'

'You heard Keri. Now maybe you'll take no for an answer.'

They both jumped, Keri most of all. When she spoke, it was with no idea that Ben was within earshot, although he probably thought her declaration was as much for him as for Rick. 'Haven't you got work to do?' he asked Rick.

'If I hadn't, you'd think of something,' Rick shot back. But he sauntered away, head down, his boots scuffing patterns in the dust as if he was mentally kicking Ben all the way back to the homestead.

Relief made Keri sag against the fence. 'I'm glad you arrived when you did.'

His brows met in a frown of disapproval. 'I thought you told me you would keep away from Rick until the wedding.'

'Too bad you didn't tell him the same thing,' she rejoined.

'I will, tonight at dinner,' he vowed. 'In the meantime, I've brought you this.'

She took the small box he held out to her and opened it. Inside was the most stunning ring she had ever seen. A Cabochon emerald in the same deep green as the waters of Crocodile Creek glowed in a setting of diamonds and yellow gold. Overwhelmed, she stared at it.

'Go ahead. Put it on.'

'I couldn't. It's far too valuable.'

His mouth twisted into a sardonic smile. 'I wouldn't have thought you'd consider its value a problem. It's an heirloom, passed on to me by my grandmother.'

The veiled insult barely registered, or perhaps she was growing accustomed to hearing them from him. 'She obviously intended you to give this to your wife,' she demurred.

'Which is precisely why I'm giving it to you.'

It would add weight to their supposed engagement, but she didn't want to compound the lie by wearing it. She held the box out to him. 'Buy me something cheap. It will do the same job.'

His eyes held a dangerous glint. 'It would be a dead giveaway—unless you want Rick to find out. Is that it?'

Her hair haloed around her head as she shook it decisively. 'Of course I don't.'

With a satisfied smile, he closed the trap. 'Then wear the ring.'

When she made no move to comply, he took the jewel box from her stiff fingers, opened it and removed the ring. With his eyes fixed on her face, he lifted her hand and slid the ring on to her engagement finger.

'There, now we're officially engaged.'

A lump rose in her throat and threatened to choke her. Such a beautiful ring was meant to seal a real engagement, not a sham like theirs. So that he wouldn't see her distress, she turned away and held her hand up to the light while she pretended to admire the ring. 'It's lovely. Thank you.'

'And you needn't worry about giving it back,' he said gruffly. 'It's yours to keep.'

Her eyes flew wide. 'I wouldn't dream of keeping it.'

'Am I so repulsive to you?'

In truth, it was the opposite which made her determined to return the ring. It would make a shambles of her intention to keep him at arm's length if she had such a tangible reminder of him after they parted. 'I wasn't thinking about you,' she denied. 'I was worried about the value of the ring.'

He arched an eyebrow. 'You surprise me. I told you I didn't expect you to co-operate for nothing. Consider the ring your payment.'

'For doing what I didn't want to do in the first place?' she asked, hurt by his words but determined not to let him see how much.

'If you like.' Without warning, the cynical mask dropped away to reveal such unhappiness that she was shaken. 'I know it must be difficult for you to stay here and see Rick marry someone else, but I'm grateful that you agreed to do it for Robyn's sake. Now I don't know if I did the right thing by suggesting it.'

She had never seen Ben like this before, vulnerable and willing to admit that he could be wrong. He was, but not in the way he thought.

The silence grew but Ben made no move to leave. He seemed to have something else on his mind. She waited for him to speak. After a while, he did. 'Let's go for a drive before dinner. I have something to show you.'

She understood his reasoning. To the rest of the family, it would look odd if they didn't spend some time together. It wasn't because he wanted to be alone with her. 'All right,' she said, her depression projecting into her voice.

'It was an invitation, not an order,' he said, sounding irritated.

'If it wasn't, I wouldn't have accepted,' she assured him. On an impulse, she touched his arm then let her hand drop as she recognised the danger in such intimacies. 'Can't we try to be civil to each other, for Robyn's sake if not for our own?'

'For Robyn's sake,' he echoed, but she couldn't tell from his tone what he thought of the idea.

They drove in silence for several miles across the unending plains, their surfaces corrugated after the long dry season. Most of the rivers had dwindled to a series of billabongs with dry river bed in between. They crossed several of these, lurching down one side and up the other at angles which made her feel as if they could tumble backwards at any moment. Ben was a skilful driver, however, and was in full control of the powerful vehicle. 'Where are we going?' she asked after their third creek crossing.

'To see a pet project of mine,' he informed her. He gave her no more clues. Her curiosity was piqued as they drove into a settlement on the banks of a creek which she recognised as part of Crocodile Creek.

She made her own assessment of the pens, buildings and fenced-off stretch of riverbank. 'You're farming crocodiles.'

He nodded. 'I've had a permit for several years, but this is the first year I've been able to put so much time into making it work.'

She didn't try to mask her pleasure. 'Crocodile-farming has been a hobby-horse of mine since . . .' She let her voice tail off. 'I'm forgetting, you've been keeping tabs on me in Darwin.'

'Enough to know you've written several articles for Australian Natural History magazine on how managed farming of crocs can help the conservation cause. One of your pieces gave me the idea to try it here.'

She was inordinately pleased. She had long been an advocate of egg-ranching and had helped to collect the eggs from wild nests so that they could be incubated under ideal conditions and the young raised on farms under special licence. The need to monitor the areas from which the eggs were taken was the reason for her survey of Crocodile Creek but she hadn't guessed that Ben was the holder of the licence, nor that he shared her enthusiasm for the idea. 'Show me everything,' she insisted.

Their differences might not have existed as he took her on a tour of the project. Large sheds accommodated the generators needed to run the incubators where the eggs were hatched. 'We have two spares for back-up in case the main one fails,' he explained.

'What's your survival rate?' she asked with brisk professionalism.

'Eighty per cent of hatchlings,' he informed her with evident pride. 'We had some trouble getting the young crocodiles to start feeding, but now they're supplied with warm, clean water, heat lamps around each pen, and a diet of fish, beef, chicken and vitamins.'

They reached a fenced-off stretch of dark water flecked with leaves and floating twigs. Patches of reeds rimmed the man-made billabong. 'What's in here?' she queried.

'My pride and joy.' He opened a metal locker alongside the pen and lifted out a pair of fat, very dead mullet which smelled ripe in the oven-like heat. At the sound of the locker opening, a prehistoric head lifted out of the reeds. It was shaped like an elongated triangle with yellowed teeth each as long as a man's finger, overhanging the jaw. As the great head lifted, its dark, noduled body emerged from the water.

Ben had attached the fish to a long pole and he held it out over the pen. With a lightning-fast movement, the cavernous jaws closed over the fish and the crocodile sank from sight beneath the water.

The leafy pool was soon tranquil again and Keri released the breath she had been holding. 'He must be at least fifteen feet long.'

'Sixteen and female,' Ben supplied. 'I'm going to find a mate for her and raise my own eggs right here.'

'Have you been in touch with the Commission? We might be able to help you locate a mate for her.'

He inclined his head. 'The Conservation Commission has offered to help, but I'd rather do things my way.'

Which explained why she hadn't heard any talk about his project at headquarters. 'Still the independent type,' she breathed softly.

'Always,' he confirmed. 'I don't believe in calling on the government for everything.'

'I hope you'll let me help at least,' she offered, adding, 'in a private capacity if not an official one.'

He looked pleased. 'I was hoping you'd offer. You're the only person I know whose enthusiasm for crocodiles is a match for mine.'

His comment was absurdly warming. To cover her reaction, she said, 'What about Rick? Isn't this his land?'

'It will be. The farm straddles both properties but he hasn't shown any interest so far. Luckily he has plenty of acreage left for whatever he decides to farm.'

'What makes you so sure he'll take to any kind of farming?'

His mouth tightened. 'I'm not. But the choice wasn't mine to make.'

Her surprise was ill-disguised. 'I thought the land was left entirely to you.'

A shadow darkened his even features. 'Remember, I was with Dad when he died. He felt badly about changing his will in my favour but by then it was too late. He begged me to sign Casuarina over to Rick when he married. I'm sure he believed Rick would have settled down by then.' His gaze was filled with irony. 'You didn't know that when you gave Rick, up, did you?'

'I suppose it's no use saying it wouldn't have made any difference to me?'

He shook his head. 'None at all.'

It was late by the time they headed home and the sun had begun to paint the mountains with red and blue haze. As the light faded outside, the atmosphere in the vehicle became more intimate. She felt emboldened to ask, 'Ben, why didn't you ever marry?'

His hands tightened on the steering wheel. 'I might have done once, but it didn't work out.'

'What happened?' she asked, her voice soft.

His expression became distant and he spoke as if to himself. 'She let me down badly. I didn't feel like trying again after that experience.'

She cast her mind back to the parade of young women who used to visit Kinga Downs when Jake was still alive. There was Persia, of course, and the secretary from Red River and a young radio operator from Katherine. A few starry-eyed jillaroos had set their caps at the Champion brothers, but Keri couldn't remember Ben showing an interest in any of them. She was puzzled. Maybe the woman he referred to had appeared on the scene after Keri left.

'What about you?' he asked, interrupting her thoughts.

'I thought you said you'd been following my exploits in the newspapers,' she challenged him.

Immediately she was conscious of a sharp drop in temperature inside the vehicle. 'What about Theo Strathopoulos?' he asked.

'What about Theo?' she asked, trying to

recapture the light mood.

But Ben was angry again for some reason. 'I suppose you're going to tell me you were just good friends?' he quoted.

'It's exactly what we were,' she confirmed. 'I met him by chance, when I was called to remove a venomous snake from his house, and we got on well from the first. Because he's a millionaire, the papers made a big deal out of it, but he was never more than a friend.'

'A rich, middle-aged one,' Ben commented, his tone scathing.

'So what,' she snapped. 'I know what you think of me, but Theo's money had nothing to do with our friendship.'

They drove on in moody silence during which she could almost hear him condemning her in his mind.

Then, without warning, he brought the car to a halt and she saw that they had reached the mile-long dam which supplied the homestead with its water. 'Feel like a swim?' he suggested.

A surge of anxiety rippled through her. She couldn't go swimming with him. 'I didn't bring my swimsuit with me,' she demurred.

'So what? You swam in your underwear often enough when you lived here before.'

But that was before, when she had nothing to hide from him. 'No, I don't want to,' she said firmly.

There was another long silence which grew steadily colder. 'Would you swim with Rick if he invited you to?'

'Of course not.'

'But you were willing to spend time with him until

I intervened.'

For a moment, it sounded almost as if he was jealous of Rick, which was crazy, surely? 'If you must know, I loathe Rick,' she confessed. 'So you see, I don't need a fake engagement to keep my distance from him.'

His mouth tightened into a grim line. 'Evidently he feels differently.'

She wrapped her arms around her body, feeling cold in spite of the heat still stored inside the car. 'I can't help what he does. I've told you how I feel. I can't make you believe me.'

His breath escaped in an explosive sigh. 'Damn it, I wish I could.'

Her head came up and she fixed him with a defiant look. 'Didn't you once tell me that a Champion can do anything he wants?'

CHAPTER FOUR

'ONLY in Australia would you think nothing of travelling hundreds of miles to buy a dress,' Keri mused, keeping her eyes on the corrugated road ahead.

Out of the corner of her eye, she saw Robyn's bouncing nod of agreement. Her glowing expression told Keri that she had done the right thing by planning this trip. She had come to Crocodile Creek with the minimum of supplies, certainly with nothing she could wear to the party Robyn was organising. Still, when Ben suggested she returned to Darwin to collect her things and take Robyn along, she was dubious.

'I'm not sure that Robyn's up to travelling by road,' she had observed.

'She has to go to the hospital for a check-up. The journey will be more leisurely and less stressful by car than by plane,' he explained. 'She's anxious enough about staying overnight in hospital. It will reassure her if she knows you're near by and you can collect her next day, after you've done your errands.'

He seemed sure she would come back. She sighed. He knew as well as she did that she wouldn't let Robyn down, whatever the temptation. 'Is there anything I can do for you in Darwin?' she asked.

He hesitated. 'No, thanks. Just take care.'

She didn't know what prompted her to ask, 'Are you sure you don't want to come with us?'

'I wish I could. But there's too much to be done here with the wet season approaching. Rick can't handle it alone.'

She understood his reluctance to leave the properties in Rick's care. 'He'll have to get used to it if he's to run Casuarina alone,' she pointed out.

A shadow darkened his expressive eyes. 'I know. I keep telling myself I should give him more responsibility.'

But he knew what would happen if he tried. 'It won't be easy for you to give up control of half of Champion Holdings,' she ventured.

He nodded distantly then shook his head as if to dismiss the notion. 'I have to do what's right.'

Yes, she thought, he would always do what was right, even if it killed him. She felt a surge of compassion for Ben who was prepared to give up everything for a cause he believed to be just. She couldn't fault him for having a conscience but she wished he wouldn't let it rule him so rigidly.

With a sigh of frustration, she turned her full attention back to the road. From the Carpentaria Highway, they had joined the Stuart Highway at Daly Waters. From here it was a straight drive north along 'the track' as the road was known, a stretch of bitumen which reached from horizon to horizon in an almost ruler-straight line.

They had decided to stop for lunch at Katherine, the first sizeable town on their route. A few miles south, they passed the turn-off to Mataranka. It would be good to stop there, Keri thought nostalgically. Years ago, she had swum in Mataranka's famous thermal pool. Set among lush palm and date trees, the pool seemed to be empty until her touch started the crystal-clear waters rippling. It was a long time since she had swum there. She couldn't imagine doing it now, among strangers who would notice what she preferred to keep hidden.

She cast a sidelong glance at Robyn who had dozed off. In sleep, her involuntary movements were stilled and she looked tranquil. She was still too thin but she looked much better than she had when Keri first arrived. The sight of her friend dozing made Keri smile. She couldn't be sorry she had agreed to stay when she saw the good her presence was doing.

The next landmark was Elsey Station, made famous by Mrs Aeneas Gunn in her book, *We of the Never-Never*. At Katherine, Keri bought barbecued chicken which they washed down with a flask of coffee supplied by Jessie that morning. They freshened up at a petrol station, where Keri had her car checked over. She didn't want to risk a breakdown between there and Darwin.

By mid-afternoon, they were pulling into the capital city. 'We made good time, don't you think?' Keri asked Robyn, who was now wide awake and interested in her surroundings. She nodded vigorously and gestured with her hands.

Keri interpreted the typing movement. 'Yes, we brought your portable keyboard. It will be the first thing I unpack.'

Her flat was in Mitchell Street, only minutes from the city centre, so they were soon making themselves comfortable there, drinking tea and stretching their cramped muscles. With access to her keyboard, Robyn relaxed, knowing she could communicate with Keri again. 'This trip was a good idea,' Keri said. 'If I'd stayed away much longer, I'd have had to send for some more clothes anyway.'

At the mention of clothes, Robyn reached for her portable keyboard. 'Party dress?' she wrote, adding several question marks.

'I know. I intend to buy one,' Keri said and laughed. Robyn's question marks were the equivalent of anyone else's nagging. 'You wouldn't let me go back without one. What are you planning to wear, anyway?'

'Sexy black silk pyjamas,' came the typed response and Robyn chuckled wickedly.

Keri's eyes gleamed. 'I see. When did you arrange to have them made?'

Robyn's hands danced over the keyboard. 'Mail order. Collect from boutique tomorrow.'

'I can't wait to see them,' Keri said. She studied the business card Robyn handed to her. It belonged to an exclusive fashion boutique in Smith Street. 'I might find something there for myself,' she speculated.

After they had washed away the dust of travel, both figuratively and literally, for the Northern Territory's infamous 'bulldust' got into every pore, Keri drove Robyn to the hospital. 'I'll be back for the evening visiting-hours then I'll collect you tomorrow to drive home,' she assured her friend.

Robyn rolled her eyes in mock resignation then she reached for her keyboard which Keri had set up on the nightstand. 'Did you see that new intern? Dishy!' with lots of exclamation marks.

Keri laughed. 'You're incorrigible.' But she was relieved that Robyn was coping so well. She felt much better as she left the hospital and returned to her parked car.

She had been looking forward to an evening to herself and had made plans to enjoy it. Suddenly none of them appealed any more, and she faced the fact that she missed Ben. At Kinga Downs she could watch him ride by from the homestead veranda, or catch a glimpse of him bent over his desk in his office. The eyes which met hers in the driving-mirror went wide with surprise. Surely she wasn't falling for him all over again despite the hazards? He still thought of her as a gold-digger. The ring she wore which he had offered her as payment for her co-operation was ample proof.

In annoyance, she slammed her palms against the wheel. Why did he insist on casting her as the villian? She understood why he was so anxious to have Rick married and settled. Jake's will had left him more or less responsible for his half-brother, but Ben must know by now that she wasn't going to sabotage Rick's plans. There had to be another explanation for Ben's behaviour towards her.

She steered carefully in the gathering dusk but her mind was only half on the driving. Ben had offered her a businesslike marriage, so he wasn't afraid of commitment. What else could there be?

Still lost in thought, she parked her car outside, ready to visit Robyn later, and took the lift to her floor. The doors had barely closed behind her when she became aware of a man lounging outside her front door. 'Rick! What are you doing here?'

'Surprise, surprise,' he drawled. 'Ben told me you were bringing Robyn for her check-up. I couldn't leave you alone in the big city at night, so I've come to take you out to dinner.'

'Ben needs you at home,' she said, her mind whirling.

'Ben doesn't need anyone. Besides, he thinks I'm still at the muster camp with the men.'

She made no move to open her door. 'You were sure I'd welcome you, but I don't. You're the last person I want to see.'

He looked pointedly around the hallway. 'Ben isn't here now, you don't have to pretend.'

'I'm not pretending,' she said, enunciating each syllable with great care. 'I don't want to have anything to do with you. Is that plain enough?'

He straightened, his eyes dark with anger. 'It's plain enough all right, but it's a different tune from the one you used to play with me. I intend to find out why.'

'Maybe I grew up and saw you as you really are,' she said tiredly. 'You're totally irresponsible. Your behaviour today proves it. And you still haven't learned how to take no for an answer.'

Rick seemed about to say something more when they both heard the phone start to ring inside her flat. 'Aren't you gong to answer it?' he queried.

Rather than open her door while he was still here, she was tempted to let it ring, but it could be the hospital calling about Robyn. She had given them this number in case of emergency. Reluctantly, she unlocked her door.

She wasn't quick enough to prevent Rick from following her inside. To her dismay he beat her to the phone and picked it up. 'Hello? Yes, this is Keri Donovan's number. Who is . . .' He stared at the instrument for a moment, looking puzzled. 'He hung up.'

A feeling of dread assailed Keri. 'He? Who was it?'

'It sounded like Ben.'

Her heart sank. It probably was Ben. He had said he would call this evening to make sure they had arrived safely. He would have recognised Rick's voice and thought they had arranged to meet in Darwin. 'How could you?' she said to Rick, cold fury in her voice.

'Steady on, I didn't know it would be Ben. You're not the only one in the soup. Now he knows I've skipped out on the muster.'

'You would think of yourself first,' she seethed. 'Get out of here before I call the police and have you arrested.'

Ben's call must have rattled him more than he was admitting because he agreed to go, asking only to use her bathroom first, which she could hardly refuse. Then he left with alacrity. She was sure her threat alone wouldn't have made him go so readily.

The evening passed with agonising slowness. Apart from her visit to Robyn at the hospital, she spent the time pacing the flat, willing the telephone to ring. If Ben called back, she could explain what Rick was doing here. For some reason, it was suddenly important that she make Ben understand that she hadn't betrayed his trust by arranging to meet Rick here.

When she could stand the suspense no longer, she picked up the phone and dialled Kinga Downs. Jessie Finch answered. 'I'm glad you had a safe journey. I know you can handle the outback but I was worried how Robyn would cope with the trip.'

Keri made herself curb her impatience. 'She's fine. She slept most of the way. I've just come back from visiting her and they tell me the check-up is routine.'

'You've set my mind at rest. I'll tell Mr Champion when he comes in.'

'Isn't Ben there?' she asked, dismay colouring her voice.

'He came in for dinner then left again. I don't know what got into him but he was furious when he drove away.'

Keri bit her lip. 'You don't know what was the matter?'

'No, but it seemed serious.'

'Did he say when he'd be back? I really need to talk to him.'

'He didn't tell me that either. All I can do is give him a message when he comes in.'

With that, Keri had to be content. It was late by the time she gave up waiting for Ben to call back and went to bed. She slept fitfully and awoke as the first light of dawn stained the sky with red. Piccaninny daylight, the aborigines called it. Baby daylight, the birth of a new day. It was an apt description, but its beauty failed to cheer her as she contemplated facing Ben tonight. He would be even more convinced that her word was worth nothing. She tried to tell herself that his opinion didn't matter but she was still troubled.

As she picked at her breakfast of toasted muffins and coffee there was a knock on her door. Her first thought was that Rick was back but it was too early. He liked to sleep late, especially after the sort of night she was sure he would have had in Darwin. It was more likely to be one of her neighbours, keeping an eye on her flat. She opened the door and got the shock of her life. 'Ben!'

'It's me,' he said grimly and marched past her into the flat without waiting for an invitation. He came to a halt in the living-room and looked around.

Suddenly she knew what he expected to find. 'Rick isn't here,' she said flatly.

'Then you don't deny that he answered your phone last night?

'Why should I? I have nothing to hide.'

'How can you be so blatant about it? You broke our agreement and spent the night here with him . . .'

'I did neither,' she broke in. 'He turned up out of the blue and barged in. You Champions make a habit of it, it seems. He picked up the phone before I had a chance to answer it. And he left two minutes afterwards,' she finished in a voice which dared him to contradict her.

She half expected him to argue but he tilted his head back and closed his eyes, massaging the sides of his neck with both hands. When he looked at her again, the light of battle had left his eyes. 'I get the feeling that an apology might be in order.'

'It would be a start,' she said evenly. At the sight

of his tired gesture, some of her anger had ebbed away and she began to realise how glad she was to see him. As usual they were on a collision course, but this time she had won. He believed her and was even willing to apologise for misjudging her. Unaccountably, she felt her spirits soar.

He took a step towards her. 'I'm sorry for thinking what I did about you and Rick last night. I should have realised he would do something stupid like this.'

She inclined her head. 'Apology accepted. Would you like some breakfast?'

The hungry way he looked at the coffee-pot was all the answer she needed. She poured him a cup and gestured to him to join her at the breakfast bar as she put more muffins into the toaster. 'Would you like me to cook something? An omelette or bacon?'

'Toast is fine. I probably don't deserve that much.'

If it came to a toss-up between arrogance and humility, she thought she preferred his arrogance. A contrite Ben Champion seemed like a contradiction in terms. 'I told you I accept your apology. There's no need to grovel.'

He tilted an eyebrow at her. 'Was I grovelling?'

'It was a good approximation.' She buttered the muffins lavishly and pushed a plateful towards him. 'There's Vegemite or honey,' she said, indicating the jars. He spread two of each and bit into a black-coated Vegemite one. She waited while he ate, then asked, 'Why are you prepared to believe me this time, when you've always thought the worst of me in the past?'

He regarded her tiredly. 'I wanted to believe you before, but you haven't made it easy for me.'

Playing with her knife, she nodded reluctantly. 'I suppose you're right. I did give the impression that the inheritance was more important to me than anything else, but it wasn't.'

'What about Theo Strathopoulos?' he asked in a low voice.

Her thick lashes curtained her expression. 'I didn't go out with him for his money. He's a charming man and I enjoyed his company.'

'But you didn't marry him.'

'There was never any question of marriage. His family is more important to him than anything. I always knew that he would be expected to marry someone from his own background. We were friends, that's all.'

'Yet he gave you all those presents,' he said, his tone accusing.

'Yes, and he got them back the next day. Showering women with gifts is Theo's way of paying them attention. I didn't accept any of the things he gave me, no matter what the papers reported.'

Ben dropped his knife with a clatter. 'Damn it, you tell me that now, but you must see how it looked from the outside.'

'I know exactly how it looked,' she said. 'I had to live with the sly glances and the gossip. That's why I stopped going out with Theo. Knowing what you think of me, I hardly expect you to understand.'

'Oh, but I do understand. What I don't understand is why it matters to me.'

Her eyes flew wide. 'Does it?'

'It shouldn't.' His voice dropped to a hoarse whisper. 'I shouldn't give a damn what you do or who you see, yet I came here ready to strangle Rick, and you for encouraging him.'

Her hand went to her throat as if to protect it. She told herself he wasn't here out of love, but only to ensure that she kept away from Rick. 'You've done your duty. You can go now,' she assured him with as much dignity as she could muster.

His expression became strained. 'I should go, shouldn't I?'

It was hard to swallow for the lump in her throat. 'Yes.'

He made no move towards the door. Instead, he took a step closer, holding his arms rigidly at his sides as if he was fighting the urge to open them to her. 'Tell me to go and I will.'

Her lips moved soundlessly, forming the words, but no amount of willpower would force them out. He should go. If he stayed, she would only get hurt again. But a longing more powerful than all the common sense in the world stilled her tongue. Helplessly, she shook her head.

The gesture was enough. Swift strides brought him to her and he crushed her against the hard wall of his chest. His fiery breath fanned her forehead and she felt the hot pressure of his hands on her back through her cotton housecoat. She swayed against him. 'Oh, Ben.'

He gasped. 'Say it again. You make my name sound like a poem.'

She nuzzled her cheek into his shoulder. 'Ben, Ben, Ben,' she repeated, feeling joy well up inside her.

He cupped the back of her neck, tilting her head up so they pressed more closely together. 'Again.'

Laughter trilled through her. 'Ben, Ben, Ben, Ben.' The chant became increasingly husky.

Then he silenced her with a kiss which gave and demanded all at once. Gladly, she accepted the gift of his mouth and returned it in full measure.

His tongue flicked along her lower lip, teasingly erotic, and she gave it a playful nip. His eyes flashed fire. 'Two can play this game,' they warned her and he clasped her lip between his teeth so that she opened her mouth in surprise. He was ready, plunging inside until she felt as if she would burst with pent-up passion.

While he continued to play love games with her mouth, she slid her hands down his shirt, opening the buttons as she went, then spread her hands across his hard mid-section. She heard his sharp intake of breath. 'Dear God, Keri.'

He wanted her, she was well aware by now. And, by all the saints, she wanted him. No amount of reason could outweigh that knowledge. When he urged her backwards on to the couch, she offered no resistance.

Like a sleepwalker, she saw him shrug off the shirt she had opened to the waist. Next, he slid his jeans off. Soon her housecoat was the only barrier between them and she helped him undo it so it fell open, exposing her to his heavy-lidded gaze. 'My beautiful Keri,' he said, devouring every inch of her with his eyes. 'You should have made me go.'

Speaking was an effort. 'Would you have gone?'

'Probably not. But it would have been better for both of us.'

Better because this was all he was offering her, she thought wildly? Yes, but no matter, she answered herself. For too long, she had denied herself this because it would lead to more pain. Yet nothing could hurt as much as sending him away.

Suddenly, all reason was drowned in a torrent of sensation as he joined her and began a leisurely exploration of her body which drove her almost wild. When she could stand it no longer, she clasped her hands along his backbone and pulled him against her in an unspoken gesture of surrender.

'Soon, my love, soon,' he murmured into her ear. Soon felt like forever and a moan escaped her throat. At the animal sound, he raised himself on one elbow and looked down at her. She marvelled at his control. 'Now, please,' she urged, sounding almost prim, as if she had said 'pass the salt'.

'Patience is a virtue,' he reminded her. But there was nothing virtuous in the kiss he pressed on to her parted lips. One knee was between her thighs and she clasped it, feeling his teeth grind against hers as a jarring response shook his whole body.

How could she have lived without Ben for so long, she asked herself. Coming back hadn't proved her resistance to him, but showed her lack of it, she acknowledged now. At least, that was how it was turning out.

Dimly, she became aware of the telephone ringing but she ignored it as she trailed kisses across Ben's stubbly chin. He seemed content to ignore it too, until they both said at the same moment, 'It could be the hospital.'

She gave a groan of frustration. They were supposed to call and arrange for her to collect Robyn, but why did it have to be now? 'I'll get it,' she said resignedly.

He pressed a finger to her lips. 'No, I will. Don't move until I get back.'

His weight shifting off her felt like a betrayal and she watched him with hungry eyes as he followed the ringing sound and disappeared into her study. The ringing stopped and she heard him speaking. The mere sound of his voice sent a shiver down her spine. Hurry back, she implored silently.

'Was it the hospital?' she asked when he came back into the room.

'Yes. You're to collect Robyn at noon. Everything is fine.'

But it didn't sound fine, she realised with a shock. His voice had lost its caressing tone. He sounded almost cold. She struggled upright and pulled her housecoat over herself. 'What's the matter? Is something wrong?'

'Not with Robyn.'

'Then what? Ben, what is it?'

In hurt bewilderment, she watched as he pulled his trousers on. Then he handed her a piece of paper. 'This was on your desk, beside the phone.'

Confused, she stared at the paper. It was a cheque for a large sum of money, drawn on the Champion Holdings Account. It carried Ben's printed signature and was countersigned by Rick with yesterday's date. And it was made out in her name. 'You can't think I'd accept money from Rick,' she asked, knowing that it was exactly what he did think.

He fastened his shirt with quick, angry movements. 'Why not? It isn't the first time I've paid off one of his *inamoratas*.'

'But I'm not one of them. I sent him away last night. Nothing happened.'

His look raked her. 'Like nothing was about to happen just now, I suppose? Well, at least I got my money's worth.'

She had never felt so cheap or degraded. The glorious feelings of a moment before were crushed into ashes. 'How can you think such things, far less say them?'

He looked at the cheque she still held in trembling fingers. 'How can I not?'

She felt sick at the sight of it. Rick must have planted the cheque in her study when he used her bathroom. She hadn't looked in there since last night, never dreaming that Rick would choose such a vicious means of revenge for sending him packing. Ben would never accept that she hadn't lied about Rick's presence here last night.

'Take this with you,' she said, holding the cheque out to Ben.

He ignored it. 'Keep it. You earned it this morning.'

Then he was gone. She stayed where she was, too heartsick to move. She should have listened to her own injunctions and kept Ben at arm's length, then none of this would have happened. As it was, she didn't know how she was going to face him again.

*   *   *

As it happened, she wasn't given the chance. Two days later, on the day of Robyn's party, Ben still hadn't put in an appearance at the homestead. From Nugget Malone, they heard that he was at the muster camp with the men.

'He is coming?' Robyn typed on the keyboard in her bedroom when Keri went to help her get ready.

'Of course he is. This is his big night too,' Keri assured her with more conviction than she felt. Surely he wouldn't hurt Robyn because of what he thought Keri had done?

She helped Robyn to dress in the black silk pyjama outfit they had collected from the boutique before leaving Darwin. Although her heart wasn't in it, Keri had also found an outfit for herself. As she stood behind Robyn, styling her hair, her glance went to the mirror. Keri's outfit was classic in design and consisted of a flowing shirt in coral silk over slim-fitting trousers of the same material, fashionably cropped above the ankle. 'Fantastic,' Robyn had typed when she saw Keri in the suit.

Keri didn't feel fantastic. She felt miserable. She and Ben had been on the verge of a truce until Rick had ruined everything with his incriminating cheque. Rick hadn't been around since they got back either, or Keri would have given him a piece of her mind. He was probably leaving his return until the last minute so that the presence of Robyn's guests would prevent her from speaking her mind.

She glanced at the clock. The first guests were due to arrive by private plane in less than an hour. Nugget was already on his way to the airstrip to meet them. Guests from the neighbouring properties were driving over and despite Robyn's promise, there would be quite a crowd. Many of the guests would stay at Kinga Downs overnight to save themselves the long trip home late at night.

In the kitchen, Jessie and a positive army of helpers were preparing what seemed like a mountain of food. Most of it came from the property's own herds and fields. Knowing that it was all being done under false pretences didn't make Keri feel any better as she watched everyone rushing around.

She wanted to get into her car and drive as far away from Kinga Downs as possible. How could she stay and let all these people celebrate an engagement which was pure hypocrisy? If the occasion hadn't done Robyn so much good, she would have left by now. But the sight of her friend's glowing expression and the encouraging reports they had received from the hospital after Robyn's check-up made Keri determined to see the night through. But where was Ben?

Leaving Robyn to finish her preparations, she escaped to her own room to finish getting ready. As she pushed open her door, her hand froze on the handle. Further down the hall, Ben was going into his own room. It took her less than a minute to make the decision. She hurried down the hall after him.

CHAPTER FIVE

WHEN she walked in, Ben gave her a look of irritation. 'Don't you believe in knocking?'

'I need to talk to you. I didn't think you'd open the door if I announced myself.'

He paused in the act of shrugging his shirt over his head. His bare chest looked as if it were hewn from mahogany. 'Too right I wouldn't. You're too expensive for the likes of me.' He completed the movement and flung the shirt on to his bed. 'I have to get ready for the party.'

'It's my party, too,' she reminded him, 'or have you forgotten that we're supposed to be celebrating our engagement?'

'Don't remind me,' he said sarcastically. 'As a means of keeping you away from Rick, it wasn't very successful, was it?'

'It's all cut and dried to you, isn't it?' she demanded. 'Didn't it occur to you that Rick left that cheque behind precisely so you'd think what you did?'

'How could he? He didn't know I was coming to Darwin.'

'He recognised your voice on the phone. He must have put two and two together and decided to get even with me for throwing him out.'

When he remained silent, she added, 'Do you think I would have left the cheque lying around for you to find if it was genuine?'

He pulled stiff fingers through his hair. 'With you, I don't know any more. It did strike me as odd that you left the thing in plain sight.'

'Yet you didn't stick around long enough to discuss it with me.' She let out a sighing breath. 'Why don't you call Rick in here and settle the question once and for all?'

The firm muscles of his chest tautened as he became angry again. 'You'd like that, wouldn't you? Have me fling accusations at Rick when it's your word against his. As it happens he came and apologised for haring off to Darwin. He even admitted that he's looking forward to settling down on Casuarina with Persia.'

'So that's that,' she said dispiritedly. 'Well, at least I know how things stand.'

'Where are you going?' he asked as she turned away.

'To pack. Robyn is in better shape now, as I'm sure her doctor told you when you visited the hospital. There's no need for us to play out this farce of an engagement any longer.'

'I'm afraid there is.'

She froze in mid-step, disturbed by the matter-of-fact way he spoke. 'What do you mean?'

'This came for you today.' He swept an unopened letter off his dresser and held it out.

Accepting it, she saw that the envelope bore the crest of the Conservation Commission of the Northern Territory. 'What is this?'

'When you open it you'll find that you've been seconded to my crocodile farm to help me overcome some problems I'm having hatching the eggs at the correct temperature.'

'But you're not . . .' she began then her voice tailed away as she understood what he was up to. 'You manufactured this so-called problem so I have no choice but to stay.' She gave him a look of appeal. 'What I don't understand is why? I thought you'd be anxious to get rid of me.'

'Robyn needs you,' he said flatly.

The thought that he might have wanted her to stay was quashed as she realised that his concern was for his sister. Voices reached them from the living-rooms, indicating that the party was already under way, and she gave a sigh of defeat. 'I'd better finish getting ready. Robyn will wonder where I am.'

At the door, he stopped her. 'Keri?'

She turned and her awareness reawoke to the fact that he wore only his trousers. She felt an absurd urge to run her hands across his chest, and dismissed the notion as crazy. 'Yes?'

'How would it be if I had a talk with Rick after the party? I know he can be a bastard at times.' He frowned. 'I haven't called him that for years. I used to catch hell from Dad for saying it. He always said it wasn't Rick's fault that we had different fathers.'

She was fairly sure what life must have been like for Ben since his father died. He must have felt enormously guilty about being left the whole of the Champion empire. No wonder he tried so hard to redress the balance. Still, she felt moved to say, 'It wasn't your fault, either. You don't have to keep trying to make it up to him.' Fearing that she had said too much, she fled from the room.

By the time she finished doing her hair and make-up, the party was in full swing. At least fifty people were clustered in the living-rooms and out on the veranda. Knowing Robyn, another fifty had been invited and would arrive as the evening wore on.

Catching sight of Keri, Robyn gestured for her to join the group around the computer console. She fixed a smile on her lips as she recognised two of the people talking to Robyn. 'Mrs Redshaw, isn't it? And Daphne, I hardly recognise you now, you're so grown up.'

The neighbour's younger daughter was many years Keri's junior and had been in pigtails the last time they met. The chatted for a few minutes and Keri discovered that Persia Redshaw was still nursing her grandmother but would be home in a few more days. 'Rick will be pleased to hear that,' she said, inwardly adding that it wasn't too soon for her, either. She glanced around. 'Where is Rick?'

'I suppose he feels left out, without Persia being here,' Mrs Redshaw said indulgently.

Keri didn't bother telling the woman how her future son-in-law had been consoling himself. 'I suppose so,' she agreed and excused herself to circulate among the other guests. Many of them remembered her from the days when her father was with the Aerial Medical Service. Repeatedly, she explained that her father and mother were both well and were living in North Queensland now.

As she talked, her glance was drawn repeatedly to the french doors leading into the room. At last the entrance darkened as Ben's substantial figure filled it. Her heart gave an unexpected leap. Without even realising it, she had been waiting for him to appear.

She went to his side, aware of eyes following her progress. At the same time, she felt a quite unwarranted surge of pride knowing that as far as the others were concerned she had every right to monopolise him. She beckoned for him to bend so that she could speak into his ear. 'I owe you an apology for what I said just now. I had no right to interfere in your family life.'

'Don't apologise,' he returned. 'I took my time coming down because I was thinking over what you said. You could be right. Maybe my guilt over being made Dad's heir did blind me to a few things where Rick's concerned.'

'All the same, I had no business interfering,' she restated.

He looked down at her hand possessively gripping his arm, and covered it with his. 'We'll talk later.'

Ben's promise made it easier to get through the evening. There was still no sign of Rick but half the district had turned out for the party. 'You said you'd keep the numbers down,' she hissed to Robyn halfway through the evening.

Robyn swung her chair around to the keyboard and typed out, 'So sue me.'

Keri regarded her fondly. In the last few days, a little colour had returned to her cheeks and she had gained a few pounds in weight. The pale, gaunt creature who had greeted Keri when she arrived had thankfully almost vanished.

A steely-haired man saw her talking to Robyn and came over to join them. 'I don't know your secret but I wish I could bottle it to give to all my patients,' he told Keri.

'I take it you're Doctor Syme,' Keri guessed. 'Robyn's told me a lot about you.'

'And all I hear about is Keri this and Keri that,' he said, laughing. 'Still, I can't fault your results.' He checked to see that Robyn's attention was held by another guest, then leaned closer. 'Before you came, it was touch and go whether we had to put her in hospital.'

Alarm showed on Keri's face. 'She's all right now, though, isn't she? She's looking better.'

'Looks can be deceiving,' the doctor informed her. 'She's fine as long as she continues to make progress. A woman with Robyn's problems needs more than the average will to overcome them. Losing her personal carer triggered a bout of depression which left her very run down. It will take her a while to get back where she was.' He patted Keri's hand. 'You're good for her, my dear. Keep it up, that's all I ask.'

Her eyes clouded, but she was careful to keep her party smile in place as the doctor walked away.

She had asked Ben not to make an official announcement about their supposed engagement, but she had reckoned without Robyn's good intentions. A little before midnight, Doctor Syme stood up and proposed a toast to 'the happy couple'. Keri wished the floor would open up and swallow her. Instead, she was forced to accept the good wishes of the guests who also offered Ben their congratuations.

He was the picture of the happy fiancé as he shook hands and bent his head for the ladies' kisses. Then he moved to Keri's side. 'Smile, this is a happy occasion.'

'It's difficult when you feel as much of a fraud as I do,' she hissed back.

'I told you, I'm quite willing to make it real,' he said equably. She could have strangled him. He knew she didn't want a business arrangement for a marriage, so he was quite safe in renewing his offer.

'You might have told me the doctor was still worried about Robyn,' she said over the rim of her champagne glass. 'You didn't have to manufacture a problem at your crocodile farm. I would have agreed to stay.'

'In that case there's no problem, is there?' he said with maddening mildness.

She felt like a bone being pulled this way and that between two dogs. Didn't she have any say in this? Angrily she put her glass down. 'If that's all the festivities, I'll say goodnight.'

Before he could respond she went to Robyn and whispered her goodnights. 'Thanks for a lovely party,' she said, squeezing her friend's hand.

Robyn nodded her pleasure and her cheeks glowed. But close up, Keri could see that the doctor was right. Robyn's flushed face didn't quite hide the violet shadows rimming her eyes, or the hollows which still marked her cheeks. Whatever Ben's reasons for keeping her here, Keri was suddenly glad she didn't have to leave just yet.

Alone in her room at last, she kicked off her shoes and moved over to the window. Beyond the veranda, the gardens were illuminated by moonlight. Palm trees laden with green bananas stood like sentinels over the display of orchids and bromeliads which were Robyn's pride and joy. Bougainvillaea, poincianas and mango trees flourished in the garden. Still, the oasis barely managed to hold back the limitless night.

Opening her doors wide, Keri sniffed the fragrant air. The steamy night reminded her of a rich woman's bathroom in which the moisture-laden atmosphere was redolent of countless expensive scents.

The party noises floated up to her and she heard the guests calling their goodnights as they walked across the gardens to the guest cabins, or retired to various parts of the homestead.

Soon, there was only the drone of the mosquitoes broken by the occasional shrill cry of a curlew in the paperbark trees. She began to relax. This was the Kinga Downs of her girlhood, the magical place she had returned to in dreams while she was studying to become a ranger.

Leaning against the doorpost, she had a vision of herself as a teenager, carefree and guileless. She had been completely taken in by Rick's charm, taking a long time to see him as he really was. She thought she had realised her mistake in time and had tried to tell Ben how she felt. But it was too late. By then he was convinced she had switched her affections because of Jake's will.

The moonlit garden reminded her of other moonlit nights when it was too hot to sleep. With Ben and Rick and some of the teenage children of the stockmen, she had gone down to the dam to cool off in the mile-long stretch of fresh water which supplied the homestead. Fed by an underground spring, it was always cool and clear.

At first she had been afraid to swim in the dam for fear of crocodiles, but Ben had assured her that there were none lurking in the shadowy, pandanus-fringed waters. 'Only the Johnston River crocs,' he had explained. The freshwater crocodiles only grew to six feet or so in length and were harmless to humans. It was the larger, more ferocious salt water crocodiles she had to fear.

Goaded by the others, she had dived into the water, keeping her legs well up in case Ben was wrong. But he wasn't, and she had come to love swimming in the cool green water. The teenagers, black, white and brown, swam in the minimum of clothing and she soon forgot her shyness at stripping down to her underwear, revelling in the feel of the silken water enveloping her.

When had that sense of ease vanished? It came to her that it was on the night she told Rick that she was going away to university. Like Ben, he had accused her of leaving because of the will, and nothing she said had made any difference.

She shuddered as she recalled how he had tried to kiss her, to show her what she was missing, as he put it. When she resisted, he had clawed at her clothing so that her blouse slipped down around her shoulders.

Alarmed by his behaviour, she had run into the bushes behind the house to wait for Rick to come to his senses. Then had come the moment she would remember for the rest of her life.

As she hid in the bushes, a bullwhip had whistled through the air out of nowhere. She could still hear the snap of its tip as it caught her across her bare shoulders. The shock of the blow had robbed her of the power to scream and her legs had collapsed under her. As she went down, a man's outline had etched itself on her brain.

There was no way she could tell anyone what happened without admitting what Rick had tried to do, and her pride wouldn't let her do that. She had made it to her room without anyone seeing her, and had concealed her injury under a sweater. Next day, her father had come to take her home, accepting her explanation that she felt she was in the way in the aftermath of Jake's death. Her parents must have been puzzled as to why she never suggested going back to Kinga Downs but they never queried her decision.

Today, the sight and sound of a man wielding a bullwhip was enough to make her flesh crawl as she remembered the hideous feel of the rawhide slicing through her shoulder.

As the memory of that experience came crowding back, the scar she still carried began to prickle and she rubbed it absently. She had managed to bury the memory of that night out of reach of her conscious mind. Why had it chosen tonight of all nights to surface again?

She glanced at the bed which one of Jessie's helpers had turned down invitingly, then she looked back at the garden. Thinking of those carefree swims in the dam had made her long for a cooling dip now. There was no one around. Dared she risk a swim in the homestead pool?

Suiting the action to the thought, she changed and was soon tiptoeing through the now silent house. The pool was located behind the house where it was only overlooked by the family room and living-rooms. Most of the bedrooms were on the other side of the house.

Quietly, she let herself out on to the terrace and took in a deep breath of pure pleasure. How inviting the pool looked, silvered by moonlight and dappled by the shadows of surrounding trees.

Jake had wanted the pool to look as much like a natural billabong as possible. Spear grass and pandanus grew nearly to the water's edge, disguising the man-made shape. At one end there was a jetty made of old timber beams. This was used for diving and sunbathing, and had been a favourite spot with the teenagers at Kinga Downs.

At the shallow end, the pool tapered into a natural-looking pebble beach where one could stretch out on the hottest day. Green slate rimmed the pool and spilled on to ochre-coloured paving stones. More timber logs and lattice had been used to form a pergola where one could sit comfortably in the shade.

Since her return, she had watched Robyn exercising in the pool and had envied her the freedom to enjoy the water. Several times, Keri had been tempted to change into a swimsuit and join Robyn, but she didn't want to face the questions she knew her scar would provoke.

Now there was no one to see it. With a sense of liberation, she shed her towelling robe at the poolside. Then she arched her arms over her head and dived into the inviting water.

Feeling as free as a water nymph, she swam up and down a dozen times then turned over and floated on her back, staring up at the myriad stars dotting the dark blue canopy overhead.

'Enjoying yourself?'

The shock of hearing Ben's voice almost made her

sink. Spluttering, she recovered and looked around to find him sitting on the timber jetty, watching her. His face was in shadow but there was no mistaking the broad set of his shoulders or the proud carriage of his finely sculptured head. To her horror, she realised that he was dressed in swimming trunks and intended to join her in the pool.

It was an effort to keep her voice steady. 'I didn't know you were there. I was just about to get out.'

He seemed to sense her reluctance to be there with him. 'Don't leave on my account,' he said. Then he jack-knifed off the jetty, cut a clean swathe through the water with his body, and surfaced a short distance away from her.

It was all she could do not to hoist herself out of the pool and huddle in her protective robe, but she reminded herself that he couldn't see anything in the moonlight. Her secret was safe for the moment.

Nevertheless, she tensed as he swam up to her and hooked his arms around the edge of the pool. 'This reminds me of when we were kids, swimming in the dam. Do you remember?'

She made herself relax, taking slow deep breaths before she answered. 'It was thinking about those days which gave me the idea to swim now.'

'Are they gone for ever?' he asked. His voice was dreamlike but she detected an undercurrent of tension. For some reason, her answer was important to him.

'I don't know,' she answered truthfully. 'I guess we all have to grow up eventually.'

'More's the pity,' he agreed. In the dappled light, she could feel his gaze on her. 'But you grew up more than most of us, Keri. You used to be so full of fun.

You couldn't wait to get into the water at every opportunity, yet I haven't seen you use the pool once since you've been back.'

'As you say, I've grown up,' she said, aware of the brittle quality in her voice but unable to supress it.

He noticed it and turned over so that he was achingly close in the balmy water. 'It's my fault, isn't it?'

'Does it have to be anyone's fault?'

'In your case, yes. I have a feeling if I'd given you a different response when you came to me after the reading of Dad's will, things would have been very different.'

'You did what you thought was right,' she suggested. 'You always do.'

He swore softly under his breath. 'But you didn't fight very hard to make me change my opinion of you. It was almost as if you wanted me to think what I did.'

She forced a laugh. 'Why should I do that?'

'I don't know. Maybe you're afraid of what a union between Rick and yourself might have produced.'

His explanation for her behaviour was so wide of the mark that she almost laughed aloud. 'How did Rick get into this?'

'You were in love with him once. Maybe you still feel the same, but with Robyn's disabilities on our side of the family and your sister's on yours, the odds in the genetic lottery can't be very appealing.'

'Is that why you think I gave Rick up?'

'Well, isn't it? If you don't care about the inheritance, as you say, then what other explanation is there?'

There was the most obvious one—that Rick

couldn't compete with the attraction she felt for Ben. She had been dazzled by Rick at first and hadn't seen the truth herself until it was too late. The genetic problems hadn't even crossed her mind. 'For an intelligent man, you sure are blind,' she muttered under her breath. Before he could react she had climbed out of the water and wrapped her robe protectively around herself. 'I've had enough,' she said, meaning it in more ways than one.

'Keri, wait,' he called and started to haul himself out of the pool. Soon he would be between her and the house. On impulse she ducked into the shelter of the pergola but he soon caught up with her there.

Moonlight dappled the space between them as he came closer. 'Keri, I know how you feel about Rick but he's no good for you, can't you see that?'

His hands rested lightly on her shoulders but she felt crushed as if under a great weight as he turned her to face him. 'It isn't Rick I care about,' she insisted.

In the moonlight his face was all harsh planes and angles. 'Then why did you come back?'

'I've been asking myself the same thing,' she admitted. 'I know when I was much younger, I was dazzled by his personality and his generosity, but I don't feel anything for him now.'

'Most of his so-called generosity was at Dad's expense,' Ben put in wryly. 'It made him see that Rick would ruin Champion Holdings, given a free hand. As it is, he's already spent every cent of the money Dad left him. If it wasn't for what I hold in trust for him, he'd be broke by now.'

'Surely that's what your father feared when he drew up his will?' she said. 'He can't have meant you to hand over Casuarina unless you were sure Rick was ready.'

In the dappled light, she saw his eyebrows arch in surprise. 'Are you telling me you don't care whether Rick gets the land or not?'

She gave a sigh of impatience. 'I'm telling you I don't care what Rick does, period.'

'But you didn't come back until Rick's wedding was announced. I was sure he was the reason.'

'Will you listen to me for once?' she demanded angrily. 'I did come back because he was getting married— because I thought that made it safe for me to come.'

In the dappled light she saw his face crease with puzzlement. 'Safe? What do you mean?'

She bit her lip. She had already told him more than she meant to. 'It's water under the bridge now,' she said dismissively. 'I thought Rick wouldn't be convinced I hadn't come back to him, unless he was safely married.' The thought made her smile wanly. 'I didn't realise you would be the one to need convincing.'

'Let's say I might have acted a little hastily.'

His hands on her shoulders pressed more tightly, bringing her closer to him. His body was damp from the swim and she could feel every masculine contour of him against her. While they talked, her robe had drifted and now he pushed the fabric further apart. His damp chest hairs teased her sensitive skin.

What had happened to her plan to keep him at arm's length? There wasn't even that much space between them as excitement stirred inside her. She had been so sure she was Ben-proof by now that she had let her guard down and he had wasted no time in stepping inside it. In his arms, it was hard even to remember why she had no business being there. She tried to remember that he had hurt her twice and she would be a fool to let him do it again. But the fool in her kissed him back, seemingly oblivious of the risks.

She was so lost in the magic of his caresses that she didn't notice her robe slipping off her shoulders until his hands began to wander over her back. She felt him go rigid as his fingers met the scar tissue on her shoulders. 'My God, who did this to you?'

Hastily she pulled the robe up again. 'It's nothing, just an old scar.'

He pulled her against him so that he could inspect the scar. 'Nothing be damned. I know the mark of a lash when I see it. Who did this to you?'

No, her mind cried the protest. Why did he have to ask her now, when the answer could destroy the fragile rapport they had finally begun to establish?

'Was it Rick?' he demanded when she remained silent.

She shook her head. 'I can't tell you.'

'Then who?'

'Leave it alone, Ben, please.' Pushing past him, she stumbled out of the pergola and fled around the edge of the pool back to the house.

In the sanctuary of her bedroom, she closed the door and bolted it. She was just in time. A few moments later he came knocking and insisted that she open the door. 'I want to know who hurt you,' he said through the timber.

Hysterical laughter bubbled up in her throat but she fought it, afraid of waking the rest of the household. If he only knew, she thought wildly, if he only knew.

The more
you love romance . . .
the more
you'll love this offer

FREE!

Mail this heart today! (see inside)

**Join us on a Harlequin Honeymoon
and we'll give you
4 free books
A free bracelet watch
And a free mystery gift**

118 CIH FAVU (U-H-R-09/89)

IT'S A
HARLEQUIN HONEYMOON—
A SWEETHEART
OF A FREE OFFER!
HERE'S WHAT YOU GET:

1. **Four New Harlequin Romance® Novels—FREE!**
   Take a Harlequin Honeymoon with your four exciting
   romances—yours FREE from Harlequin Reader Service®. Each
   of these hot-off-the-press novels brings you the passion and tenderness of today's greatest love stories . . . your free passports to
   bright new worlds of love and foreign adventure.

2. **A Lovely Bracelet Watch—FREE!**
   You'll love your elegant bracelet watch—this classic LCD quartz
   watch is a perfect expression of your style and good taste—and it
   is yours FREE as an added thanks for giving our Reader Service
   a try.

3. **An Exciting Mystery Bonus—FREE!**
   You'll be thrilled with this surprise gift. It is elegant as well as
   practical.

4. **Money-Saving Home Delivery!**
   Join Harlequin Reader Service® and enjoy the convenience of
   previewing eight new books every month delivered right to your
   home. Each book is yours for only $2.24*—26¢ less per book than
   the cover price. And there is *no* extra charge for postage and handling. Great savings plus total convenience add up to a sweet-
   heart of a deal for you! If you're not completely satisfied, you may
   cancel at any time, for any reason, simply by sending us a note or
   shipping statement marked "cancel" or by returning any shipment to us at our cost.

5. **Free Insiders' Newsletter**
   It's *heart to heart*®, the indispensible insiders' look at our most
   popular writers, upcoming books, even comments from readers
   and much more.

6. **More Surprise Gifts**
   Because our home subscribers are our most valued readers, when
   you join the Harlequin Reader Service®, we'll be sending you ad-
   ditional free gifts from time to time—as a token of our
   appreciation.

START YOUR HARLEQUIN HONEYMOON TODAY—JUST
COMPLETE, DETACH AND MAIL YOUR FREE-OFFER CARD

Get your fabulous gifts
ABSOLUTELY FREE!

MAIL THIS CARD TODAY.

GIVE YOUR HEART
TO HARLEQUIN

YES! Please send me my four Harlequin Romance® novels FREE, along with my free bracelet watch and free mystery gift. I wish to receive all the benefits of the Harlequin Reader Service® as explained on the opposite page.

PLACE
HEART STICKER
HERE

NAME _____
(PLEASE PRINT)

ADDRESS _____ APT. _____

CITY _____ STATE _____

ZIP CODE _____

118 CIH FAVU (U-H-R-09/89)

OFFER LIMITED TO ONE PER HOUSEHOLD AND NOT VALID TO CURRENT HARLEQUIN ROMANCE® SUBSCRIBERS.

HARLEQUIN READER SERVICE® "NO RISK" GUARANTEE
— There's no obligation to buy—and the free books and gifts remain yours to keep.
— You pay the low members-only discount price and receive books before they appear in stores.
— You may end your subscription anytime by sending us a note or shipping statement marked "cancel" or by returning any shipment to us at our cost.

START YOUR
HARLEQUIN HONEYMOON TODAY.
JUST COMPLETE, DETACH AND MAIL YOUR
FREE OFFER CARD.

If offer card is missing, write to: Harlequin Reader Service® 901 Fuhrmann Blvd
P.O. Box 1867 Buffalo NY 14269-1867

CHAPTER SIX

AFTER a long time, she heard Ben return to his own room. Shakily, she changed out of her damp swimsuit and into her nightdress but sleep refused to come when she lay down.

So much had changed since she went to the pool, herself most of all. While she had been holding herself aloof from Ben, some part of her was longing to be in his arms.

It should be an object lesson in how vulnerable she still was to being hurt by him, but her mind preferred to dwell on the feel of his hard body against her, and the warmth of his kiss as he plundered her mouth. She could have told him the truth about the scar, using it to drive a wedge between them again. So why hadn't she done so? Could it be that, despite the risks, she wanted him to care about her?

More confused than ever, she tossed and turned, finally falling into a restless sleep.

She couldn't have been asleep more than a couple of hours when she was disturbed by a knock on her door.

Groggily, she peered at the bedside clock. Ben knew what time she had gone to bed. He wouldn't waken her now unless it was an emergency. But when she stumbled to the door and unlocked it, Rick was waiting outside. 'What is it?' she asked, feeling a surge of alarm.

'Relax. I'm not here to cause trouble. Some of the stockmen were night-fishing down at Crocodile Creek and one of them was attacked by the rogue croc. Since you've been monitoring them, Ben thought you ought to know.'

'Where is Ben now?'

'Getting some gear together. Then he's going after the crocodile.'

She didn't hesitate. 'Give me two minutes to dress and I'll come with you.'

'But Ben said you were to stay here.'

She had a swift vision of Ben pitting his strength against the prehistoric monster she had been studying and a shudder shook her. She couldn't let him face that alone. 'I don't care what he said. I'm coming and that's that.'

She closed the door on Rick, enjoying his open-mouthed reaction. Then there was no time to think. Shedding her night clothes, she left them in a heap on the floor and pulled on her khaki ranger's shirt with its distinctive shoulder patches. Her brown shorts, socks and work boots came next. They felt hot and constricting against her skin but she wasted no time worrying about it. She had to be with Ben.

He was loading up the Range Rover when she came out. 'What are you doing here?' he demanded.

'My job.'

'The hell you are. Go back to bed, will you?'

'Sorry, no. This is what I trained for. You won't have to worry about me,' she promised.

In the half-light, he gave her a searching look, his eyes clouded as if he was fighting a battle with himself. 'All right, get in,' he conceded.

She did so with alacrity, hoisting the last of the gear up with her. Ben closed her door then took the driver's seat. Soon they were bumping across the paddocks that led to Crocodile Creek. Two more station cars moved into convoy behind them.

In the insect-splattered vehicle with the dark green bush crowding in on all sides, she was suddenly conscious that they were alone together. Rick had tried to come with them until Ben assigned him to another car. Now she found herself wishing that at least one of the men had come with them.

'What happened?' she asked, to fill up the silence which stretched uncomfortably between them.

'It seems that Nugget's brother, Ningara, was the one attacked. Luckily the croc latched on to his catch rather than the man. He was pulled off balance into the water and got a hell of a fright, but the croc was so busy with the fish that Ningara had time to climb up the bank to safety.

'Thank goodness,' she said, heartfelt. If the crocodile hadn't been so interested in the barramundi which was one of its favourite natural foods, the outcome would have been tragic.

'It looks as if Fang will have to be moved before someone is taken,' she added.

Ben shot her a sidelong glance. 'Fang?'

'It's the name I gave to the crocodile with the damaged jaw,' she explained. 'He's most likely to be the one causing the trouble.'

'It couldn't possibly be the female,' he said, his tone sarcastic.

'Females aren't always the troublemakers,' she

said, well aware of his train of thought.

'You could be right,' he relented. 'We'll see whether Ningara's description of his crocodile matches your Fang.'

'If it does, what will you do then?'

'You said he wouldn't be dangerous if he had a steady food supply. I could keep him as a mate for Matilda.'

It was an inspired idea. 'He'd be perfect,' she enthused. 'From my observations, he's in good condition, apart from his jaw, and he's of breeding age. It would certainly be a better solution than moving him to a new location, then having him turn up again in a few months' time.'

'Which solves the crocodile problem at least,' Ben said in a low voice.

'What other problem is there?' she asked. Even as she said it, she remembered and was glad he was too involved in the driving to see the colour which surged into her face.

'I still mean to find out who hurt you,' he confirmed. 'How can you protect someone who'd do such a thing?'

'It depends how much you care for that person,' she said carefully. 'In any case, it's in the past now. Why is it so important to you?'

His fingers tightened on the steering wheel. 'Because I . . . because you're important to me.'

A lump rose in her throat. If only he was saying it because he truly cared, and not because of the good she could do for Robyn. She looked steadily out of the window, blinking furiously.

She was relieved when they finally drove up to the

clearing at Crocodile Creek. It was light enough to see without torches. On the riverbank, a group of stockmen clustered around a seated figure whom she recognised as Ningara. Even from there she could see he was recounting his adventures in great detail. No doubt it would be the subject of a grand corroborree in due course.

Talking to Ningara soon confirmed that Fang was the crocodile which had attacked him. 'He's a plenty big kinga,' he confirmed. 'Better you catch him soon, boss.'

Thanks to Keri's observations, they already knew most of Fang's movements so they were spared the task of tracking it by spotlight over several nights. They could start choosing the best trapping sites in the mangroves straight away.

After helping him clear several passages through the mangroves, Ben's stockmen clustered around while he explained how the crocodile trap worked.

It was a simple socklike net with a bait at the narrow end and a noose around the entrance. 'When the crocodile grabs the bait, he releases a weight high up in a nearby tree. This comes down and closes the noose on the crocodile,' he explained while they nodded thoughtfully. Keri was already familiar with the method and she found herself focusing on Ben's expressive hands and the richness of his voice as he briefed his men. It was an effort to keep her mind on the task at hand.

The men were less enthusiastic when it came to setting up the trap. This had to be done at low tide so that the trap was submerged when the water rose. By the time the trap was set, everyone was covered in mud and eaten by mosquitoes and sandflies. Using repellents was out of the question as the crocodile's acute sense of smell would detect any hint of chemicals.

'What happens now?' she asked Ben as they brushed the caked mud off their legs.

'We leave the trap unbaited for a couple of days so Fang gets used to it. Then we bait it with a few pounds of wild pig or a nice juicy flying fox.'

She became aware of Ben's gaze intensifying as he looked at her, and she felt immediately self-conscious. 'Is something the matter?'

'It's you. Out here, in the middle of an operation like this, you seem different somehow.'

She looked around but the men were all busy at their appointed tasks. 'In what way?' she asked.

'As if this is the most important task in the world to you,' he managed after a thoughtful pause.

'It is,' she agreed. 'What's the matter? Doesn't it fit your image of me as an unscrupulous gold-digger?'

When he winced, she saw she was right. 'Maybe I did jump to a few conclusions. I accepted your word about the cheque, didn't I?'

'That was big of you,' she muttered under her breath and swung away to see how the trap was coming along.

He caught up with her at the edge of the mangroves. 'You can't blame me for thinking you were after the main chance. You did turn up here as soon as word got out that Rick was to get ownership of Casuarina.'

'All right, I planned the whole thing,' she said in a

defeated tone. 'I would have married Rick if he'd been named as Jake's heir. I couldn't bear the thought of him marrying someone else, so I came back here like a shot to try to win him back. Are you satisfied now?'

As she became more emotional, her voice rose and she saw the men giving them amused glances. Ben took her elbow and pulled her close to him. 'You aren't making this easy, are you?'

'I thought I was,' she said with exaggerated innocence. 'I've just confessed, haven't I?'

'How should I know?' he growled. 'You're as changeable as the wind. I don't know what to make of you any more.'

Her hair flew around her face as she tossed her head. 'I don't believe you ever did.'

Several days later, they returned to the creek with a haunch of wild pig to use as bait. This time, Ben planned to camp at the creek until the crocodile took the bait. When she made it clear she was staying too, he was less enthusiastic.

'There's no need, I can have one of the men keep a watch,' he insisted.

'I need to be here to tranquillise the animal so it doesn't get overstressed,' she countered.

His frown grew blacker. 'And what about you getting overstressed?' But he didn't offer any more arguments against her presence.

Perhaps it was the screech of an egret, put to flight by Fang's thrashing, but she awoke as day broke over the creek, instantly alert and sure that something was about to happen.

The rest of the camp was still sleeping. She dressed quickly and quietly then made her way to the creek to check on the trap.

The morning was utterly still except for an occasional rumble of thunder across the northern sky. The monsoonal rains would soon arrive and flood these lush green banks. Until then, there was no relief from the oppressive heat, and the air was so moisture-laden she could almost taste the dampness.

Pulling aside the curtain of pandanus palms, she swept her gaze across the cool green expanse of river. The surface was undisturbed except for a gnarled log drifting slowly downstream.

The log changed course suddenly and she realised that it was a big crocodile, easing its way towards the bait. Her heart hammered painfully against her chest as she watched and waited, hardly daring to breathe.

A light touch on her shoulder almost sent her crashing down the bank but Ben's hand clamped around her, steadying her. She gestured towards the river and he looked, then nodded. She felt his body go rigid as he saw what was happening. Her attention was torn between the awareness of Ben's closeness and the drama playing itself out at their feet. She shut out the first sensation although her nerve-endings throbbed in response to his touch. Still she felt a resounding gladness that they were sharing this special moment.

Then it happened. In a blur of movement, the giant crocodile lunged forwards and clamped its jaws around the bait. The sound of flesh tearing made her shudder and Ben's grip tightened.

The force of the crocodile's attack triggered the mechanism which jerked the snare taut. Ben had used industrial webbing which wouldn't cut or choke the animal and now it tightened around the armoured girth. The resistance it provided would gradually exhaust the crocodile. As it rolled and thrashed, she caught a glimpse of its lower law. 'It's Fang!'

They had to wait several hours until the animal was tired enough to attempt an approach. Keri kept watch on it until she judged the time was right to administer a tranquillising shot. As soon as the Flexadil began to take effect, Ben brought his men in with ropes to winch the crocodile up the bank to the waiting trailer.

The muscle relaxant made the animal safer and easier to handle, but they kept a wary eye on the huge jaws until Fang was safely aboard the trailer.

She and Ben had been working side by side since the moment of capture, anticipating one another's needs as if they were in telepathic contact. When Nugget slammed the tailgate shut on their prize, Ben grabbed her and swung her high into the air. 'We did it! By God, we did it!'

Her sense of elation matched his. 'We sure did. They'll be calling you Bring 'em back alive Champion after this.'

His eyes danced. 'More like Bring 'em back alive Donovan. You did all the scientific stuff.'

'We're a great team,' she said, smiling, then sobered as she realised how true it was. Since dawn they had worked together like two halves of a perfect whole. She had worked on captures like this, but never in such harmony before. Her lowered lashes fanned her hot cheeks. 'Today was fantastic, wasn't it?'

He had also turned serious as if his thoughts echoed hers. 'Fantastic,' he agreed. Then his voice lifted. 'Let's just hope Matilda likes Fang.'

The intimacy which had existed a moment before vanished. She tried to make her tone as light as his. 'You know how it is with arranged marriages, they'll learn to love each other.'

'Can you learn to love?' Ben asked in an oddly brittle tone. 'I thought you either did, or you didn't.'

She shrugged. 'Who knows with crocodiles?' But she had a feeling that he wasn't talking about the saurians.

Ben had prepared a second pen next door to Matilda. They had a moment of anxiety when the time came to remove the topes trussing Fang, but the crocodile was still affected by the muscle relaxant and moved sluggishly when he discovered that he was free.

The stockmen moved back smartly, aware that a blow from the massive tail could break a man's legs. But it was some time before the animal recovered enough to move at its old speed, then it made for the artificial pond covered with lilies and sank beneath the surface. Soon all they could see was the distinctive nostril ridges and the bulbous eyes.

'That's it, show's over,' Ben announced.

She felt a stab of disappointment that the adventure was ended. She was pleased that the crocodile had survived the relocation in apparently good health. A lot could go wrong, from infection setting in to drowning, while the crocodile was drugged. Luckily nothing had gone wrong. No one had been hurt, although that was always a possibility in such dangerous work. They had much to be thankful about.

Still, she felt depressed, reluctantly recognising that it was because the closeness she had shared with Ben had also ended with the adventure. Today they had moved and thought as one, and she knew she would miss the feeling for a long time.

Ben didn't seem to share her mood. He was still on an emotional high after the capture and she watched him laughing and joking with his men. When he spoke to her it was with an easy friendliness which should have cheered her but only made her feel worse.

She didn't want to be Ben's friend, she discovered with a sense of shock. She wanted to be much more.

For the next few days she came out to the crocodile farm with Ben to see how Fang was settling in. There was no question of introducing him to Matilda until he was at home in the new surroundings. 'Has he eaten yet?' she asked Nugget on one such visit.

'No, not yet,' the stockman admitted sorrowfully. 'I've tried all the crocodile tucker I can think of, from flying fox to haunch of buffalo. He just lies there sulking.'

She and Ben exchanged worried looks. 'If he doesn't eat soon, we'll lose him,' Ben said for both of them.

They had the same idea at the same moment. 'What if he heard us feeding Matilda?'

There was no reason why it should work but nothing else had, so Ben decided to give it a try. As soon as he opened the bin holding Matilda's supply of fish, her giant head rose out of the lilies and the great jaws snapped open, waiting. Ben fed her slowly, making the production as noisy as possible. Then he hooked a dead mullet on to the end of the feeding pole and held it out over Fang's pen.

They held their breath. Very slowly, the water parted and two eyes appeared, fixed on the mullet overhead. Then Fang lifted his head out of the water and closed his teeth over the fish. With a snapping sound, the fish was gone and he sank again.

Keri's sparkling eyes were reflected in Ben's. 'He's going to be all right.'

The crocodile accepted two more mullet then sank beneath the water. Because of their slow metabolism, the crocodiles fed only once a week, so this meal was more than enough to sustain Fang. Keri felt a warm glow of happiness as they walked away from the pen towards Ben's Range Rover.

Why can't it always be like this? she asked herself. Here at the crocodile farm, he was warm towards her, but the feeling evaporated when they returned to Kinga Downs homestead. There she was treated with loving warmth by everyone except Ben.

'Is everything OK between you two?' Robyn had typed on her keyboard the previous evening.

'It's fine, nothing for you to worry about,' she had assured her friend. Robyn still believed she and Ben were engaged and Keri dreaded telling her the truth. Robyn had been improving steadily since Keri arrived, but lately she had begun to look pale and listless again. Keri hoped it wasn't because of the strained atmosphere between herself and Ben.

She was conscious of it now as they walked back to the car. Her need to be in his arms was like a hunger, growing in intensity with every day she spent here. But it would never be satisfied as long as this wall existed between them.

With her hand on the car door-handle, she paused.

'We can't go on like this.'

Ben reached around her to open the door for her. 'I know, but we don't have a choice until Robyn is a lot better. I'm sorry that it's so hard on you.'

It was, but not for the reasons he thought. 'You still think Rick's the reason I'm here, don't you?' she said tonelessly.

The muscle in his jaw worked. 'You admitted as much on the day of the crocodile hunt.'

Was that why he had been so cool towards her ever since? She thought he understood she had been provoked into saying it in the heat of the moment. 'I didn't mean it,' she insisted. 'It was a stupid thing to say, even in jest.'

His eyes darkened but whether with anger or sadness, she couldn't decide. 'Many serious things are said in jest,' he reminded her. 'I'd find it easier to believe you if I hadn't seen the marks on your back. Only blind love could bring a woman back to a man who did that to her.'

Caught between Ben and the car door, she had nowhere to run, and no way to avoid his intense gaze as he searched her face. The pain she glimpsed as he looked at her resonated inside her. 'No, Ben, you're wrong,' she protested.

He didn't seem to hear her and when he spoke, his voice was filled with anguish. 'My God, it is true.'

As he walked away from her, she thought of pursuing him and trying to make him listen to her. But what could she say when he had already read the truth in her eyes? She did love the man who had branded her, for all the good it was going to do her.

CHAPTER SEVEN

FOR the next few days, Ben kept out of her way. She began to wonder why he bothered with the pretence of an engagement, when it was obvious to anyone that they were anything but a loving couple. Then she realised that he had to go on with the fiction for Robyn's sake.

When Robyn was around, usually when they dined together at the end of the working-day, he maintained a front of loving concern for Keri. But as soon as Robyn retired for the night, he withdrew into his shell. The only time he opened up to her was when she asked him about Fang.

'He's much more approachable, especially when you come bearing food,' he told her.

At the warmth of his voice, a pang shot through Keri. She tried to tell herself that she wanted him to be indifferent to her. It would make their inevitable parting so much easier. She was surprised how hard she had to work to convince herself.

'How is Fang getting along with Matilda?' she asked, finding that she enjoyed the cessation of hostilities between them and wanted to prolong it.

He smiled but even as she responded, she saw his gaze become distant and knew that he was mentally at his crocodile farm. 'Fang seems eager to meet Matilda. Every time he sees her, he throws himself at the wire barrier separating them. The trouble is, I don't know whether he's smiling at her affectionately or hungrily.'

That's why they say, "never smile at a crocodile",' she half sang. 'Whichever it is, I've seen them mating in the wild and I'm glad I'm not a crocodile.'

He joined her in her laughter and for a moment, there were no barriers between them. Then his shuttered look told her he was remembering all that had gone before. He stood up and stretched. 'I'd better turn in. Tomorrow is a long day.'

Against all common sense, she felt a need to keep him there for a short time, prolonging the camaraderie of the last few minutes. 'What are you doing?' she asked.

A flicker of irritation crossed his face but he paused. 'I'll be down at the stock yard sorting cattle. Nugget's bringing in fifteen hundred head tomorrow. Most of them have never seen a human so you can't afford to turn your back on them for a second.'

Something sharp twisted inside her as she pictured him risking his life among a mob of wild cattle. She had a momentary vision of his husky body trampled under thousands of flailing, razor-sharp hooves and she had to bite back the urge to tell him to be careful. What he did was his own business. She should be glad that he was making this so easy for her.

'Ben,' she began, then remembered her place. 'Goodnight.'

He didn't look back. 'Goodnight.'

When she came to breakfast next morning, Ben had already gone to the stock yard. Looking out across the property from the veranda, she could see a

low-lying cloud of dust staining the sky close to the
horizon. This was the only sign that a large mob of
cattle was on the move. Most of the men were there,
either helping to move the cattle or awaiting their
arrival at the yards.

So there was only herself, Robyn and Jessie Finch
at the large table which normally seated up to a
dozen. After breakfast Jessie planned to take the
morning off, after receiving Keri's assurance that
she would look after Robyn.

'How would you like to visit Fang today?' she
asked Robyn when the meal was over.

Robyn's head bobbed up and down
enthusiastically and her grin broadened. She
welcomed any excuse to escape from the confines of
the homestead, and she hadn't had a chance to meet
Ben's newest charge yet.

A little guiltily, Keri realised she was eager to go
today because she knew there was no chance of
running into Ben at the crocodile farm.

'Ready, Robyn?' she asked as she let herself into
her friend's bedroom. Robyn was dressed in her
outdoor gear of checked shirt and moleskin trousers,
but she had wheeled herself up to her computer
terminal.

Keri moved up behind her. 'Was there something
you wanted to tell me?'

Robyn's hands roved over the keyboard, stabbing
at the specially shaped keys. 'You and Ben.
Anything wrong?' she typed out.

Keri looked at the words for a long time before she
said anything. She tried to keep her voice light as she
asked, 'What makes you think something's wrong?'

'Mood is not good,' Robyn typed back.

Tendrils of apprehension curled inside Keri. As if to make up for her disabilities, Robyn was unusually perceptive when it came to people's moods and feelings. Ben should have considered that when he manufactured an engagement between them. 'We had a disagreement,' she confessed, knowing that she couldn't pretend nothing was wrong when Robyn already knew it was. She squeezed her friend's shoulder. 'It's OK, every couple has them.'

Robyn's shoulders slumped, signalling her relief. 'Kiss and make up soon,' she typed.

Keri forced a laugh. 'Whatever you say. Shall we go now? Fang is waiting for his breakfast.'

Robyn nodded and Keri waited for her to clear the screen of its last message but she wheeled herself around and headed for the door. As Keri caught up with her and helped her manoeuvre her chair through the enlarged doorway, she caught another glimpse of Robyn's last message.

Her heart sank. How could she kiss and make up with Ben when their romance was a fraud from the beginning? Soon they would have to tell Robyn that they weren't getting married at all, but Keri wasn't looking forward to breaking the news to her.

Afraid that Robyn would sense her despondent mood, she kept up a stream of small-talk as they drove over the rutted track to the crocodile farm. 'I had a letter from Dad this morning. They know I'm staying here. My sister Louise has moved into a flat with two other girls from her sheltered workshop. Isn't it wonderful?'

Although she was deprived of her keyboard in the car, Robyn made a gesture which Keri knew meant she was pleased. 'She'd like you to write to her,' she ventured.

Robyn nodded agreement. Keri knew how hard her friend had fought to gain some measure of control over her life, so she would be the ideal person to guide Louise during her own struggle for independence. Robyn tugged her arm and made a gesture which encompassed the wide brown land around them.

'You want me to invite her to visit Kinga Downs?' Keri interpreted correctly. 'She'd love it. I've told her about the place in my letters, but it's not the same as seeing it for yourself. I'm sure Mum and Dad could arrange to bring her. Thanks for suggesting it.'

They covered the remaining miles in silence. Keri was pleased that her young sister would have the chance to see this place for herself. Robyn would be a wonderful model for Louise, who was just starting to discover her own potential.

At the same time, Keri felt a stab of apprehension. She hadn't told her family anything about her supposed engagement to Ben Champion, assuming that the charade would be over before they needed to know about it. But if the Donovans came here, they would be bound to hear about it and wonder why Keri hadn't told them. She sighed deeply. Damn Ben and his machinations.

At least she knew where she was with the big saurians, Keri thought as she wheeled Robyn up to the wire fence surrounding Fang's pool. She took a pair of dead mullet out of the bin alongside the pool and fixed them to the feeding pole, then handed the pole to Robyn. 'You do the honours.'

At the sound of the bin opening, Fang's massive head had appeared among the lilies garlanding his pool. As Robyn held the pole above his head, he opened his mighty jaws and snapped them closed over the fish. Robyn laughed in delight and held out the pole for Keri to refill it.

She did so then pushed Robyn up to Matilda's pool. The large female was waiting, having heard Fang being fed. 'You take care of Matilda while I check on the current batch of eggs,' Keri told Robyn, loading a couple of poles with fish.

Leaving her friend to feed Matilda, she made her rounds of the incubators where batches of crocodile eggs were being kept at constant temperature until they were ready to hatch.

She found Nugget checking the incubators. 'I thought you'd be out at the muster,' she commented.

He grinned, his teeth gleaming whitely against his dark skin. 'I'd rather be bitten by baby crocs than trampled by wild cattle.'

She smiled back. 'I see your point.'

At her request, he showed her the clutches of eggs which were being incubated at controlled temperatures. It was only recently that they had discovered that the temperature at which the eggs was kept determined how well the new born crocodiles survived. When they were hatched at lower temperatures, the young crocodiles looked healthy but did not survive as well as those hatched at higher temperatures. Satisfied with the readings on each incubator, she left Nugget to his work.

Making her way back to the open-air pens, she caught sight of Robyn talking to someone. Her apprehension returned as she recognised Rick.

'What are you doing here?' she asked. 'I thought you'd be giving Ben a hand.'

'I'm not Ben's shadow,' he said, irritability clouding his expression. 'He has a dozen men jumping to do his bidding. He doesn't need me. Besides, this is my land.'

As it happened she had forgotten that the crocodile farm straddled the invisible border between Kinga Downs and the outstation, Casuarina. 'Ben told me this is Casuarina land,' she responded in a neutral tone. 'But I wasn't aware that it was yours yet.'

Rick made a show of studying his fingernails. 'The papers are at the solicitor's now. The land will be mine by this time tomorrow.'

Something in his voice sent a shiver through her. He made the statement sound like a threat. 'Have you heard from Persia?' she asked, changing the subject.

He made a sound of disgust. 'Persia, Persia, Persia. She's all I hear about these days. Well, she's back at long last but her grandmother didn't make it so her family don't think it's proper to make wedding plans just yet.'

'I'm sorry to hear she lost her grandmother,' Keri said tautly.

'Yes, yes,' he dismissed her condolences. 'Ben decided it wasn't fair to keep me waiting any longer to come into my inheritance, so he went ahead and set the wheels in motion.'

Robyn stirred restively in her chair and Keri squeezed her shoulder supportively. 'Don't worry, you'll still get to have your wedding, won't she, Rick?'

He fixed her with a sharp glare. 'Are you in a hurry to have me married off or something?'

From her position behind Robyn's chair, she frowned at the top of her friend's head and back at Rick, trying to remind him that his sister shouldn't be subject to any unnecessary stress. 'Of course not,' she said, injecting a false note of cheer into her voice. 'But I know how much Robyn's looking forward to the wedding.'

Belatedly, he got her message and reached forward to rumple Robyn's hair. 'Worry you not, it will all work out. The main thing is, I'll be able to prepare Casuarina—for my bride,' he added although to Keri's ears he didn't sound over-enthusiastic. She had a feeling that the property meant much more to him than his fiancé did.

'That's good news, isn't it Robyn?' she said heartily, hoping she didn't sound as false as Rick.

She became aware that Rick was shifting from one foot to the other and his gaze kept darting to the sliprails which marked the entrance to the crocodile farm. 'Is something the matter?' she asked him.

He swung his gaze back to her. 'Nothing's the matter. I suppose you girls are heading back to the homestead now?'

Inwardly, she winced at his choice of words. 'We weren't in any hurry. Ben will be gone all day. He knows I planned to come out here and gave me permission to try introducing Matilda to Fang.'

Rick's frown deepened. 'Does it have to be now?'

'Not really. They're still wary of each other, so it may be as well to wait a little longer.'

'Good.' He saw her look of puzzlement and added hastily, 'I mean, I wouldn't want them to start fighting when we had so few men here to separate them.'

For once she had to agree with him. 'You're right, of course. I'll leave it for today. But I do want to get them together before the start of the wet season, so Matilda can have a chance to nest.'

Rick saluted her mockingly. 'Quite right, Ranger Donovan.'

She kept her smile in place with an effort. 'Cut it out, Rick. I've had about enough of your jokes.'

Rick's mouth twisted into a sneer. 'Miss Goody Two-shoes. Anyone would think you really intended to marry Brother Ben.'

Robyn's thin shoulder tensed under Keri's hand. She patted it reassuringly. 'Of course I do, Rick. What a crazy thing to say.'

'Is it so crazy? I notice you two haven't set a date for the wedding yet.'

'Any more than you and Persia have,' she retorted. She was immediately sorry that she had let him provoke her. 'You can't come between us, if that's what you're hoping. Ben wants to marry me, so you may as well accept it.'

'I know Ben wants you,' he agreed in a sly tone. 'It's the reason why I want you, too.'

'One day your jealousy of Ben is going to be your undoing, Rick,' she vowed, then slipped the brake off Robyn's wheelchair. 'Come on Robyn, let's go home for some lunch. Are you as hungry as I am?'

Robyn looked up at her but shook her head. The talk with Rick had robbed both of them of their appetites. As Keri wheeled Robyn back to the car, she was disturbed by the misery in her friend's eyes. She felt like strangling Rick.

As she steered the four-wheel-drive vehicle through the entrance to the crocodile farm, she was surprised to see another car coming the other way. It was a large sedan, its highly polished white paintwork streaked with the red dust of the outback. Inside were four men, their business suits looking out of place here. 'Do you know them?' she asked Robyn as the car came closer.

Robyn waved a hand dismissively. Slowing the car, Keri tried to get a look at the occupants of the other vehicle. Out here, strangers were a rarity and never passed without stopping to exchange greetings.

This time was the exception. Robyn slumped in disappointment as they drove past. 'It's all right, I think I know one of the men,' Keri said and swung their car around, driving back into the crocodile farm.

The men had left their car and were being greeted by Rick when Keri pulled up. 'Hello, Theo,' she called to the tallest of the men.

He looked surprised to see her. 'Hello, Keri, how are you?'

Theo Strathopoulos was almost unfairly handsome. Close to six feet tall, he had the deep barrel chest of an opera singer, and the broad shoulders of a professional fighter, with a fighter's sure movements to go with it.

Although he wasn't yet forty, his head of hair was streaked with silver, giving him a distinguished elder-statesman appearance which was a great help in his business dealings. His remarkable business acumen had enabled him to amass one of the largest personal fortunes in Australia, but Keri was sure his looks hadn't hindered him either.

'What brings you out here?' she asked, surprise mingling with pleasure at seeing him again.

Theo glanced at Rick who inclined his head ever so slightly. 'Just business, as usual,' he shrugged. 'I thought you were off in the wilds, catching crocodiles.

She spread her hands to indicate the layout around them. 'I am. This is it. Ben Champion needed some help with his egg-ranching project and the Commission gave me to him, sort of on lend-lease.'

Theo's eyes became warm as they roved over her. 'Ben is a lucky man.'

'Weren't you just leaving, Keri?' Rick asked, trying without success to mask his irritation. Clearly, he didn't want her interfering in whatever business he had with Theo and his associates. 'Robyn is waiting in the car for you,' he added pointedly.

She took the hint. 'I was about to return to Kinga Downs, where I'm staying,' she said for Theo's benefit. 'Before you go, come and meet Robyn. I've told you about her.'

Rick huffed impatiently but Theo ignored him. 'I'd like to meet her.'

As he followed her back to the car, she moved closer to him. 'What really brings you here, Theo? Crocodile-farming isn't a commercial proposition yet, so it can't be that.'

He shrugged, the gesture harking back to his Greek origins. 'Why does it have to be anything in particular? Rick Champion invited me to look over the project and here I am.'

She knew him well enough to know when he wasn't levelling with her. She also knew she wouldn't get him to tell her a word more than he wanted to. 'Here's Robyn,' she said over-brightly, opening the car door wide. 'Robyn, this is my friend from Darwin, Theo Strathopoulos. Theo, Robyn Champion.'

Tactfully he showed no surprise at Robyn's infirmities, taking the hand she waved at him in greeting and kissing the back of it with exaggerated courtesy. Robyn's smile widened and spots of colour appeared on her cheeks.

'You have wonderfully expressive eyes,' he said softly. 'It is a pleasure to meet you.'

Robyn giggled again and looked aay. Then she tugged at Keri's arm and made an eating gesture.

'Robyn wants you to come to dinner at Kinga Downs,' Keri interpreted. 'Will you come tonight, after you finish here?'

'I would be delighted,' he agreed. 'Maybe I'll finally get to meet your Ben Champion.' His eyes sparkled. 'I hear that good wishes are in order, Keri. I must also congratulate your fiancé tonight.'

She stared at him. 'How did you find out?'

He regarded her gravely. 'You should know I

have my resources. You must tell me what you'd like for a wedding present.'

'There's no need,' she demurred, horrified that the news had managed to reach his ears.

'Nonsense. This time you have no reason to refuse a gift from me. What shall it be? A beach house in Darwin? The use of my private plane for your honeymoon?'

The mention of honeymoon made the ring on her finger feel uncomfortably heavy. It was guilt, she supposed. She hated deceiving people and the story had spread far wider than she ever intended it should. Surely Ben knew by now that she wasn't going to interfere in Rick's marriage plans, so he should let her off the hook. She resolved to take it up with him at the next opportunity.

'I can see I've given you a difficult choice,' Theo said graciously. 'I'll leave you to think about it and tell me what you'd like over dinner this evening. Until then.'

He bent over her hand and then Robyn's, then returned to Rick who had been pacing up and down, watched impassively by Theo's men. She assumed that one of them was the ever-present bodyguard and the other two were business associates of some kind. Lawyers? Accountants? He said today's visit was business-related, but in what way?

His refusal to give her a clue wasn't unusual. When they were going out, he seldom discussed his work. Normally, she accepted his reticence, but this time she was burning with curiosity about his presence here. There was also a feeling of apprehension which seemed to be with her all the time lately, as if something terrible was about to happen. But what?

During the preparations for dinner, she managed to ignore her feelings of anxiety. After her day off Jessie Finch was glad to have a guest to fuss over. She and Robyn threw themselves into planning the menu, spending a good hour hunched over Robyn's computer as they went through her files.

'You could run a restaurant with the information stored on that thing,' Keri told them as she went past, her arms filled with flowers from the homestead garden.

'Sometimes it feels as if we already do,' Jessie acknowledged. 'With all the staff and visitors to this place, there isn't much of a difference.'

With the food preparations in hand, Keri busied herself setting the table with Robyn's beautiful Georgian silverware and the Crown Derby dinnerware which had belonged to Ben's grandmother.

'It looks lovely, dear,' Jessie told her when she finished. 'I hope your Theo appreciates all your work.'

'He isn't my Theo, we're just friends,' Keri asserted. 'But Theo is used to having the best, so he will appreciate what we've done.'

All the same, it wasn't Theo she found herself waiting for as the day progressed. Several times she found excuses to go out to the veranda, where she had a clear view of anyone approaching the homestead. On her fourth such visit, she caught sight of a broad-shouldered figure sitting tall atop his work-horse and her heart gave an uncharacteristic leap. Ben was on his way back.

They were in the living-room enjoying a pre-dinner drink when she joined them. His hair was slick and dark from his shower and he had changed into a white silk shirt and impeccably tailored black trousers which moulded his muscular legs like a second skin.

Her eyes roved over his tall figure. He had only been gone a day but it felt longer. It was becoming more and more of an effort to remember how much he had hurt her once, and how foolish she would be to let it happen again.

'Scotch and ice?' she anticipated his choice. When he nodded she went to the bar to make the drink, needing the activity to quiet her racing pulses and fast-beating heart. Even though she knew all the reasons why she shouldn't let him disturb her, his very presence was enough to banish them from her mind.

'What's the occasion?' he asked as he accepted the drink. Their fingers brushed for an instant and she felt a jolt like electricity arc through her.

'We have a dinner guest, Theo Strathopoulos,' she said, her voice unsteady. She saw his eyes narrow as he concluded that Theo's arrival was the reason for her nervousness. 'He's staying in the area and Robyn wanted to invite him,' she added. 'I hope you don't mind.'

At the mention of Theo's name, his gaze had hardened but he said, 'Why should I? This is Robyn's home too.'

Promptly at seven, Theo arrived. This time he was

accompanied by just one man, who Keri guessed was his bodyguard. The man declined their invitation to join them for dinner and went outside. From the windows, they saw him prowling around the homestead. Theo took no notice of him and gave all his attention to Robyn who was enjoying the chance to play hostess to someone new.

Theo was particularly interested in Robyn's paintings since he already owned some of her work. He eagerly accepted her invitation to visit her studio. But when Keri moved to accompany them, Ben touched her arm. 'Let Robyn show him around. Unless you object to him spending time with another woman.'

He was watching her, waiting for her reaction, she saw. 'Of course I don't mind,' she said. 'I've told you, Theo and I are just friends.'

'Then why is he here, if not to see you?' Ben asked with a hint of steel in his voice.

She glanced towards the door, tempted to tell him her suspicions about Theo's presence on Casuarina land. But Robyn could come back at any moment and, without more to go on, she couldn't risk upsetting her friend in her present state of health. She bit her lip. Ben would just have to go on thinking the worst for now.

CHAPTER EIGHT

FOR Keri, the dinner was a tense affair, despite the efforts of Robyn and Jessie to make it enjoyable. Most of the food had been grown or raised on Champion land. The centrepiece was a huge sirloin of beef spit-roasted to mouth-watering tenderness and served with a vast array of home-grown vegetables and salads.

The menu included Jessie's famous pumpkin soup and a fish course of Moreton Bay bugs, miniature lobster-like crustaceans which were barbecued to crisp succulence. Then followed the traditional Australian dessert of Pavlova, a frothy meringue filled with tropical fruits and freshly whipped cream.

It was a meal fit for a sultan but Keri was too preoccupied to do it full justice.

'Not hungry, Keri?' Theo asked, finally noticing her lack of appetite.

She pretended to be full. 'I've eaten so much since I came here that I'll have to go on a diet when I leave.'

She recognised her slip of the tongue as soon as she saw Ben frown. If she was really marrying him, there would be no question of her leaving. But Theo didn't appear to notice the slip. He patted her slim stomach with a familiar gesture. 'What nonsense. A voluptuous woman is all the more desirable, don't you agree, Ben?'

'Perhaps.' Ben's face was as dark as thunder. He wasn't to know that Theo communicated as often by touch as by speech. Fleetingly she wondered why he should care what went on between her and Theo, then she realised that he wanted to keep up appearances for Robyn's sake.

Feeling guilty that she had momentarily forgotten how important their relationship was to Robyn, she deflected her interest on to Ben. 'What do you think is the ideal shape for a woman?'

'Perhaps you should look in a mirror to refresh your memory,' he said with such intensity that she was startled. If he was play-acting for Robyn's sake, he was excelling himself.

Theo lifted his wine-glass in a toast. 'An excellent suggestion, Keri.'

She glared at him. Why was Theo deliberately flirting with her in front of Ben? He knew as well as she did that there was no romance between them. She was relieved when Theo announced that he would have to take his leave.

Following him into the hallway, she grabbed his arm. 'What were you playing at in there?'

Her angry whisper left him unmoved. 'I don't know what you mean.'

'Yes, you do. You were trying to make Ben jealous—and succeeding,' she added grimly.

He smiled. 'After tonight, maybe he will show you the appreciation which you deserve. You see, I do love you, Keri, as a cherished friend. I want the best for you.'

'Ben is the best,' she hissed back, glancing over

her shoulder. But he was still in the dining-room talking to Robyn.

'In that case, I apologise.' Theo lifted her hand and kissed the back of it, his eyes dark as they met hers.

It was unfortunate that Ben chose that moment to walk into the hall. His sweeping glance took in their joined hands and Theo's smouldering gaze. At once, Keri snatched her hand back and realised how much worse the gesture made things look. 'I was just saying goodbye to Theo,' she gabbled.

'I can see that,' Ben said coolly.

'Forgive me for taking liberties with your bride-to-be,' Theo said, not sounding in the least apologetic. 'I claim the right as an old friend, to thank you for a superb evening and wish you both every happiness in future.'

Ben muttered a response and Theo left. No sooner had the door closed behind him than she caught the force of Ben's simmering rage. 'That was a very touching scene. Watching it, one could easily forget you were engaged to me—or is that what you were trying to do?'

'Actually, Theo was trying to make you remember it,' she said tartly, stung by his attack. 'He thought you weren't paying me enough attention. Of course, he doesn't know that the whole thing is a sham.'

A frown darkened his features. 'Thank you for the timely reminder. But you needn't worry, it won't be necessary for much longer. Persia Redshaw came home yesterday.'

'Yes, I know,' she volunteered then could have

bitten her tongue off. She hadn't told Ben about meeting Rick and Theo at the crocodile farm.

He was quick to pick up her slip. 'You saw Rick today?'

She could hardly deny it. 'He came to the crocodile farm while we were feeding Fang and Matilda.'

His eyebrows tilted upwards. 'We?'

'Robyn and me,' she supplied. 'Did you think 1 arranged to meet Rick alone at the crocodile farm?'

'Why not? You knew I would be tied up all day.'

'Well it wasn't like that,' she denied hotly. 'I didn't know Rick would turn up. As it happens, the first thing he told me was that Persia was back. I could hardly seduce him while we were talking about his fiancée, could I?'

He shook his head. 'I suppose not. Anyway, it explains why you wanted to see Theo again.'

'Explains what?' she asked, confused now.

'You know there's no chance of reconciliation with Rick, so you asked Theo here out of pride.'

'Then you know more about my motives than I do,' she threw at him. Then she shot a guilty glance towards the dining-room, and made an effort to lower her voice. 'I asked him here as much for your sake as mine, to find out what he's doing in the area.'

He frowned, deep in thought. Then in the next bewildering minute, he caught her in his arms and pulled her against him, moulding his lips to hers in a fiercely passionate kiss. Instantly, her body yielded to his mastery and all her plans to be aloof and distant with him blew out of the window. She felt a fiery warmth surging through her and she began to respond almost against her will, when she heard a chuckle close behind her.

With seeming reluctance, Ben tore his mouth from hers. 'Oh, Robyn, I didn't see you there.'

Disappontment shafted through Keri. His sudden display of passion was purely for Robyn's sake. He must have heard her wheelchair approaching and decided to silence Keri in the most practical way.

She cursed herself for a fool. In another split second, she would have responded to his kiss as if it had been real, giving away the dangerous attraction he exerted over her. Realising how narrow had been her escape, she stepped away from him but the prim movement brought a fresh grin to Robyn's face. 'I didn't know you had voyeuristic tendencies, Miss Champion,' she said with mock severity. Over Robyn's head, she glared at Ben. He had no right to fuel Robyn's belief in their supposed romance when they would have to tell her the truth soon.

Outside, a car horn sounded and Ben straightened. 'I'll let you help Robyn to bed, *darling*,' he said with heavy emphasis on the endearment, his eyes defying her to contradict him. 'That will be Nugget. I promised I'd go with him to make sure the new stock is safely bedded down for the night.'

The horn sounded again. He opened the door and called out, 'Coming,' through the opening, then looked back at her. 'Don't wait up, I may be late.'

This last was said for Robyn's benefit, she felt sure. He didn't know that Keri wanted to talk to him about Theo's visit to the crocodile farm. Since she couldn't tell him now without alarming Robyn, she said lamely, 'I won't. Goodnight.'

Left alone with Robyn, she became aware that the other woman was simmering with excitement. She found out the reason as soon as she wheeled Robyn to her bedroom.

Before the wheels of her chair had stopped turning, Robyn headed straight for her keyboard and began to type. In her excitement, her words were half-finished, leaving Keri to guess their meanings. 'Theo wants to buy your paintings?' she hazarded. When Robyn nodded vigorously, she queried, 'All of them?'

'All,' Robyn typed, adding, 'he likes Escarpment series.'

Keri also liked the series of watercolours which Robyn had been assembling for the next exhibition. Working from photographs, she had managed to capture the majesty of the Arnhem Land Escarpment in all its changing moods and hues. She hugged Robyn. 'It's wonderful news. Congratulations.'

'Thanks,' Robyn typed, ending with a string of exclamation marks to indicate her buoyant mood.

'Would you like something to help you sleep?' Keri asked, concerned about the bright spots of colour which stained her friend's cheeks.

Robyn's fingers spanned the keyboard. 'No, feel great.'

All the same, Keri was worried about the effect Theo's offer could have on Robyn's fragile health. Doctor Syme wanted her to avoid too much stress. This was positive stress, to be sure, but it could still be too much for Robyn to cope with at the moment. She tried not to let her concern show as she helped Robyn to get ready for bed.

When she returned to the dining-room Jessie declined her offer to help clear up after dinner, saying she would leave it for the housemaids to do in the morning. 'I'm off to bed,' she said, smothering a yawn.

Keri looked at the clock. It was late, and Ben had instructed her not to wait up for him. She wavered, then reluctantly went to her own room where she began to get ready for bed.

Easing her cream silk shirt off over her head, she caught sight of herself in the full-length cheval mirror which stood in a corner. Ben had suggested that she look into a mirror to see his ideal woman. He had been pretending for Robyn's sake, of course, but she couldn't help recalling the intensity with which he had said it.

In this pose, her breasts stood out high and firm, and her tanned body shone golden in the lamplight. She let the shirt drop to the floor and examined her face. Her eyes were large and luminous in this light. Although her lipstick had worn off hours ago, her lips were still bright with colour, a legacy of Ben's kiss, she thought with a rush of pleasure.

She crushed the feeling as it arose. She didn't want to connect his touch with pleasure, or with any kind of good feelings. They could be too easily taken away from her, like the last time.

So why did her body persist in vibrating with response every time she remembered being in his arms? She scrubbed at her mouth with the back of her hand but the colour refused to fade. It was as if he had branded her with his kiss, the way he marked one of his prize steers.

Annoyed with herself, she reached for her terrycloth robe, a skimpy garment which reached her thighs. It was more than enough covering in this hot climate. She swung it around her and belted it quickly. Maybe a cool shower would help banish Ben from her mind so that she could get a good night's sleep.

She stayed under the shower for a long time letting the cool spring water sluice away some of her confusion. She had agreed to pretend to be Ben's fiancée to help Robyn, not to leave herself open to fresh heartbreaks. Yet wasn't that what she was doing by letting him dominate her thoughts?

When she emerged, her hair clung to her head in tight curls and her face gleamed in the moonlight. With her robe belted over her shower-damp body, she looked like one of the Mimi, the spirit people depicted by the aborigines in their cave art, she thought, seeing herself reflected in the mirror as she padded across the floor.

Sitting down at her dresser, she started to towel her hair dry. Distantly she heard the front door open and close again. In spite of her efforts to curb it, her heart gave a little leap of response. Ben was back. Now that Robyn was safely asleep, she might be able to bring up the question of Theo's presence on Champion land.

Before she could move, there was a light tap on her door. 'Come in,' she called softly, and was annoyed at the warmth she heard in her voice. She told herself it was because she welcomed the chance to have a private talk with Ben, but the quickening of her pulses contradicted the logical explanation.

From under her turban of towel, she heard him slip into the room and close the door behind him, his masculine footfalls heavy in contrast to hers before. 'I won't be a minute,' she said, her voice muffled by towelling.

'Take your time. I'm happy to sit here and watch.'

In horror, she snatched the towel from her head. 'I thought you were Ben. Get out of my room.'

'You're not being very hospitable. You only just invited me in,' Rick observed.

She took in his ruddy complexion and the brightness of his eyes. 'You've been drinking.'

He shrugged. 'What if I have? I was entitled to a bit of fun after spending half the evening sipping tea with the Redshaws.'

So that was where he had been. Desperately, she cast around for a way to get him to leave quietly, without disturbing Robyn. 'I don't suppose they feel like drinking so soon after the loss of Persia's grandmother,' she commented.

'They never feel like drinking,' he complained. 'They don't know the first thing about having a good time.'

'Things will be different when it's just you and Persia,' she offered.

'I wouldn't know. I never see her alone long enough to find out what she's really like.'

She was aghast at this information. 'Then how can you consider marrying her when you don't really know each other?'

'What does it matter? She's female and available. As brother Ben says, it's time I did the decent thing. If I'd known that this was all it would take to get him to part with some of Dad's inheritance, I'd have married you when I had the chance.'

A feeling of revulsion overtook her. 'Don't you have any principles at all?'

His gaze swept over her, taking in the skimpiness of her robe over her dewy skin. 'Not a one, darling. Besides, it isn't a question of principles to want what's rightfully mine.'

'You mean what would have been yours if you'd shown any care for it,' she retorted. 'If you'd put in half the hours that Ben does on this property, you would have more of a claim to it.'

As she spoke, his colour grew more hectic and she began to wish she had held her tongue. He was in no condition to appreciate a lecture on responsibility now. No doubt he had heard it from Ben a dozen times since their father died.

Rick climbed to his feet and loomed over her, gripping the edge of the dresser for support. 'Just shut up,' he ordered. 'I may have to put up with this from Ben, but I don't have to take it from you.'

'Of course you don't,' she tried to placate him. 'I spoke out of turn just now and I apologise.'

He seemed hardly to have heard her. 'Not that it makes much difference now. Both you and Ben will be laughing on the other side of your faces in a couple of days.'

At the mention of Ben's name, fear gripped her. 'What do you mean, Rick? Tell me.'

Her peremptory tone cut through the alcoholic haze enveloping him. 'I shouldn't tell you, not yet.'

'But you will, won't you?' she coaxed, forcing herself to release the breath she was unconsciously holding.

'Yes, I will,' he chuckled. 'It's too late to do anything to stop it now, anyway.'

'To stop what?'

He stumbled back to her bed and collapsed on to the end of it, smiling at some secret triumph he was imagining. With an effort, he snapped out of it and focused on her. 'Theo 'n me are going to be partners in the biggest casino south of Darwin.'

Although the night was warm, her body turned icy and she hugged the robe around herself. 'Where are you planning to build this casino, Rick?' she asked, although she was afraid that she already knew the answer.

'Where do you think? Along Crocodile Creek. Theo's already checked out the site and he agrees it's perfect.'

So that was what Theo and his men were doing when she and Robyn saw them at the crocodile farm. 'What about Ben's egg-ranching project?' she asked, keeping her voice carefully neutral.

'What about it?'

'The crocodiles need a natural environment in which to breed. They won't survive with a casino on their doorstep.'

Rick's shoulders sloped expressively. 'So what? I only need a teeny bit of the land. There's a million acres out there, for goodness' sake.'

'But the farm is already established on that stretch

of the creek. It would take years to get it going somewhere else.'

'I should have known I'd get an argument out of you. All you care about are those man-eating handbags of yours.'

'They're not man-eaters,' she protested, provoked in spite of herself. 'They've been here for centuries, much longer than we have. They have a right to a protected existence.'

He waved his hand dismissively. 'Then they'll have to be protected somewhere else.'

'Does Ben know about your plans?'

'Why should he? It's my land. I can do what I like with it.'

She clutched at a faint hope. 'It isn't yours yet, surely?'

'I told you, brother Ben generously arranged for me to take it over right away, since the wedding's been held up.'

'You don't plan to marry Persia at all, do you?'

He grinned sloppily. 'If there was a way out of it, I'd stay footloose and fancy-free. But good ole Ben thought of that too. If I don't marry within three months, the deal's off and he gets the land back.'

'You've thought of everything, haven't you?' she said, despair making her voice husky. 'But I can still tell Ben what you're planning in time for him to stop it.'

His smile became sly. 'I told you, it's already too late. The only way I lose Casuarina now is if I don't make it to the altar, and I'll be there with bells on so you needn't get your hopes up.'

'Then why are you telling me all this?'

'So I can watch you squirm as the bulldozers move in. Despite my best efforts, you're still here and Ben is still besotted with you. Since I can't change that, I have to get my own back another way.'

'By raping the land and leaving nothing for your children?'

'I'll leave to them just what Jake left to me: damn-all,' he asserted. 'My kids won't be Champion stock, after all. I'm only the stepson, remember? The offspring of a gun-shearer who had a weak heart and no insurance, and a Champion bride who lost interest in me as soon as my half-brother came along.'

'I'm sure that isn't true,' she denied weakly.

'Then why did she give everything to the Champions, including herself in the end? If Jake hadn't wanted more kids, she'd have lived through that flood.' To Keri's horror, Rick's voice faltered and she saw traces of tears streaking his face.

Compassion overcame her dislike of him and she went to him, kneeling alongside him. 'Don't, Rick. It wasn't anyone's fault that she died. You can't hold the Champions or any person responsible.'

'What would you know about it?' Angrily, he pushed her away and she sprawled backwards on to the floor, her robe spilling open. At the last moment, she clutched at the cord fastening the waistline, but she still exposed a lot of tanned flesh to Rick's hungry gaze. He dropped to his knees beside her, preventing her from getting up.

'Rick, let me up, please.'

He tugged at the cord holding her robe closed.

'You were about to offer me comfort. I'm accepting your offer. What's wrong with that?'

'It wasn't what I was offering and you know it,' she protested, pushing his hands away.

'Bloody hell!' The cry burst over both of them like a thunderclap. Neither of them had heard the door open and Ben come in. Now he stood over them like an avenging angel. 'Get up,' he ordered Rick. 'You, too, and make yourself decent.'

'Ben, it isn't what you think,' she said urgently, hating the way he was looking at her. 'Rick's just had a bit too much to drink.'

His eyes raked her unrelentingly. 'That's his excuse. What's yours?'

'I don't need one. I haven't done anything wrong.'

'Not by your standards, maybe.' He gave an exasperated sigh. 'I thought you were finally coming to your senses, Rick.'

The belligerent Rick of a moment before had vanished. He leaned against the wall, looking down at his feet. 'I didn't mean anything by it, Ben. I guess seeing Persia tonight and knowing we couldn't be together yet did something to me.'

It was such a blatant fabrication that Keri gave a gasp of dismay. Surely Ben didn't think this was all her fault? But Ben evidently accepted Rick's word. 'There are more acceptable ways of working off your frustrations,' he pointed out.

It was too much! 'He didn't come in here to work off any frustration, as you put it,' she exploded. 'He came here to gloat about how he intends to destroy Casuarina.' She swung her blazing eyes on to Rick.

'Tell him what you just told me.'

He shuffled his feet uncomfortably, then gave Ben a look of appeal. 'I don't know what she's talking about.'

'Well, I do,' she countered, hands on hips. 'He plans to let Theo Strathopoulos build a huge casino on Casuarina land, right next to Crocodile Creek.'

Ben raked a hand through his dark hair. 'My God!'

'She'll tell you anything to get me in your bad books,' Rick broke in. 'But I'll bet she won't tell you how she invited me in here tonight.'

Ben's eyes narrowed and she saw his hands ball into fists at his side, as if he would like to hit someone. But all he said was, 'Did you invite him in, Keri?'

Too late, she saw the trap Rick had set for her. 'Yes, I did, but I thought . . .'

'You thought I wouldn't be back till much later,' Ben cut in.

'No, it wasn't like that. Tell him, Rick.'

'Oh, he'll tell me, all right,' Ben said coldly, earning a look of alarm from his half-brother. 'But not here. Outside.'

He accompanied the command with a sharp jerk of his head towards the veranda. Keri started to follow but Ben shook his head. 'Stay out of this.'

Her jaw dropped. How could she stay out of it, when she was already involved? But Ben was in no mood to listen to her arguments. And nothing Rick said now could make matters any worse so she slumped on to her bed.

The memory of the time when Ben had refused to

believe her over the will came rushing back, the hurt as fresh as if it were new. She had known it would be like this if she let Ben get close to her a second time. There was no comfort in discovering that she was right.

The murmur of voices reached her on the still night air. When they refused to be shut out, she moved to the window and looked out.

Ben and Rick were on the lawn in front of the house. Although they spoke in lowered tones, their voices carried.

'I thought you would stick to your deal this time.'

'Who says I haven't?'

'Your behaviour tonight.'

'I told you, she invited me in.' She cringed as Rick repeated the half-truth. Then she gasped as she saw Rick take up a fighting stance in front of Ben.

Ben reacted swiftly. 'Don't be an idiot. I can take you any time. Drunk, you don't stand a chance.'

'I'm not drunk,' Rick mumbled, but he backed away. Ben followed him and he lifted his hands. 'Don't hit me.'

'It's tempting,' Ben affirmed. 'By heaven, if I hadn't promised Dad, you'd be walking off this land for good.'

Rick straightened but still took a pace backwards. 'But you did promise, didn't you? If it had been me, I'd have stuck with the will and forgotten all about any deathbed promises. Now you're stuck with it.'

Ben's hands curled into fists and she heard him breathing hard as he fought for control. 'Don't bet on it, pal,' he ground out. Shouldering a stunned Rick out of his way, he stalked back into the house.

Feeling sick, she backed away from the window. Despite Ben's injunction that she stay out of it, she couldn't go to sleep and leave things as they were. She had to talk to him.

He was in the kitchen, filling the kettle with water, when she came in. 'I thought you were going to bed,' he said without turning around.

At least he hadn't ordered her away, she thought with a rush of relief. 'How did you know it was me?' she asked.

'The aborigines taught me how to identify people by their tread. Besides, neither Rick nor Jessie wears Louis Feraud perfume.'

His words were teasing but his tone was devoid of humour. She had heard that tone before, in firefighters when they came home from fighting a bushfire which had finally beaten them and gone on to devour thousands of acres of scrub.

'Rick lied, you know,' she said softly but with an edge of determination in her voice.

He plugged in the kettle and spooned coffee into a mug. 'I know.'

She stared at his slumped shoulders. 'You know? Then what was that performance all about just now?'

He turned around. In the harsh electric light, his eyes were ringed with violet shadows. He looked exhausted. 'I meant I know Rick wasn't entirely blameless. That's why I'd rather talk in the morning, when he's had time to sober up.'

'When he'll conveniently have forgotten everything, you mean,' she challenged him.

He massaged his eyes with one hand then dropped

the hand and looked straight at her. 'What do you want from me, Keri? An admission that I didn't see what I saw just now?'

'No, I want you to leave some room for doubt, that's all.'

He unhooked a second mug from its wooden rack. 'Want some?'

'Yes, please, very weak.' She didn't really want to drink coffee at this hour, but neither did she want to leave Ben until they had straightened this out.

She waited in silence until he had made the coffee then followed him into the living-room where he set the mugs down on a low table. Outside, all was black and still, the silence broken by the chirrup of cicadas and the occasional shrill cry of a curlew. Faintly, as the wind changed, she heard the rhythmic clicking of singing sticks and chanting as the aborigines entertained themselves in traditional fashion. The sound arose and vanished with the wind movements, making it sound ghostly. A chill rippled along her spine.

Ben caught the slight movement. 'Are you cold?'

'No, I'm fine.' The night was balmy and warm, the wind a whisper of coolness which she welcomed after the day's hot breath. 'Did you know that Rick blames the Champion family for the death of his mother?'

'Our mother,' Ben corrected, cradling his hands around his coffee mug. 'Yes, I know. What does that have to do with anything?'

She swung around, resting her hands on the back of an armchair. 'Don't you see, that's why he would sacrifice Casuarina, and why he's so keen to come between you and me.'

'I thought I was the one coming between you and him,' Ben observed with faint irony.

'You don't have to, because Rick doesn't care about me,' she said. 'He just wants to even the score between the two of you.'

Ben raked his hands through his hair. 'Do you think I don't know what drives him? He's easy to understand, and if it wasn't for Dad's wishes, I know how I'd settle it. You're the one I don't understand. You seem to understand Rick well enough, but still you keep coming back for more.'

Something snapped inside her. 'For God's sake, Ben, there's only one reason I keep coming back for more and it isn't Rick. He can't bear to see you happy, so he's out to destroy our love as well.'

She stopped, aware that she had revealed far more than she intended to. Ben was staring at her intently. 'What love, Keri? Answer me.'

'The love he thinks we have for each other,' she said weakly.

'That wasn't what you meant, though, was it? The love you meant is real, isn't it?'

'Yes,' she whispered. God help her, it was real, and he had seen it in the transparent moment when she had lost control of her emotions. Somehow, despite her vow to remain at arm's length from Ben, he had managed to get in under her guard. And now he knew it too.

He crossed the room in swift strides and gathered her into his arms. His tiredness had vanished in a second, and his grasp of her shoulders was strong and irresistible. She melted into the embrace willingly, knowing there was no point in hiding her feelings from him any longer, or from herself for that matter.

His mouth crushed hers, hot and seeking, and she yielded to its demands, becoming so much clay in his hands. She felt herself shaped and moulded to his heart's desire, even as he fused into the shape of her dream lover. 'God, Keri, why didn't you tell me?' he said, his lips moving provocatively against her mouth.

'I didn't even tell myself,' she confessed. 'I was so angry I didn't know what I was saying.'

'So the truth will out,' he noted. 'Is it the truth? Was it me all along, and not Rick?'

'Yes,' she agreed, 'it was always you.'

He would have known even if she hadn't confessed, because she was telling him with every movement of her body against his. How could there be secrets between them when their bodies were such terrible liars?

With one hand, he held her against him while the other strayed across her shoulder, pushing her robe aside so that he could kiss the inviting hollows of her throat. She heard a soft moan and realised that it came from her own throat. She twined her fingers into his hair, bringing his head down so that he could leave a trail of kisses across her shoulders. When he nuzzled her robe aside and found her right breast, she drew a strangled breath, instinctively moving her hips against him.

His teeth grazed her sensitive nipple and warmth flooded through her. She pressed his head closer and kissed the top of it joyfully. How could she have denied herself this moment in case it led to more pain?

He trailed kisses across her chest, pushing her robe aside with his head so that he could kiss her other breast. All of a sudden she became aware of a change in him, as if someone had poured icy water over their passion.

'Ben, what is it?' she asked, confused. He lifted his head and looked at her with such naked pain in his eyes that she was shaken. 'What's the matter?' she repeated.

'Go to bed. Don't argue, just go,' he ordered in a harsh undertone.

What had she done? Scalding tears of hurt and confusion sprang to her eyes but she refused to give way to them until she knew why she was being dismissed so cruelly. One minute everything had been wonderful between them, the next, he refused to look at her or explain what was the matter.

He remained immovable, keeping his back to her and ignoring her pleas, until in despair she fled back to her room.

Once there, she stood shaking, unable to believe what had happened. Something had turned Ben against her, but what?

Searching for an answer, she turned to the cheval mirror, as if her reflection could provide a clue. Then her hands went to her breasts and she slid the robe off her shoulders, finally seeing what Ben had seen—the heart-shaped birthmark surrounding her left nipple, which Rick had taken such perverse pride in describing to Ben.

CHAPTER NINE

ROBYN was wheeling herself away from the breakfast-table when Keri walked into the dining-room next morning. Her eye flew unerringly to Ben's place at the head of the table, but the jumble of plates and cutlery there showed he had breakfasted some time ago.

Robyn intercepted the glance and shook her head, gesturing towards the windows to indicate that Ben was already out on the property. Keri didn't know whether to feel relieved or cheated. She could have tried to explain how Rick came to be so familiar with her body's distinguishing marks, but she wasn't sure Ben would listen, far less believe her.

Pensively, she poured orange juice into a glass and sat down with it, ignoring the bacon and scrambled eggs keeping hot on a sideboard. She had slept little last night and had no appetite this morning.

Robyn watched her in concern then wheeled herself to her keyboard. 'You OK?' she queried on the screen.

Keri forced a wan smile. 'I'm fine. I didn't sleep too well last night—the heat, I suppose.'

'Hope so,' Robyn sympathised through her keyboard.

Not wanting to alarm Robyn unduly, Keri made an effort to brighten up. 'What have you got planned for today? Want to help me visit Fang and Matilda?'

Robyn's head swung from side to side then she reached for her keyboard. 'Sorting paintings for Theo,' she explained.

Keri nodded, relieved that her friend would be occupied today. Still, she felt bound to offer, 'Would you like me to help you?'

'Later, with the packing,' Robyn supplied. 'Drop by the studio if you get lonely.'

'Thanks, I will,' Keri agreed. When Robyn had wheeled herself out, she shared a sardonic smile with her reflection in the polished tray covers. She was supposed to be protecting Robyn from undue stress, not depending on her for companionship.

She refilled her coffee-cup twice as she thought about last night. Despite how things looked, Ben had accepted her word that she hadn't encouraged Rick. But the sight of the birthmark had been the last straw. She should have told Ben how Rick came to know about it, then he wouldn't have jumped to the most obvious conclusion. She had put off telling him for fear he would think it was a new trick to interfere in Rick's marriage plans. She should have known her silence would look even more incriminating.

An explosive sigh escaped her tightly compressed lips. She was damned no matter what she did. Ben hadn't even listened to her bombshell that Rick and Theo planned to develop Casuarina. He would never do such a thing and couldn't conceive of anyone else who would—far less a Champion. Except that Rick wasn't a Champion.

She looked up as Jessie came bustling in.

'Finished your breakfast, dear?'

'Yes, thanks, I'm not very hungry,' she explained as the housekeeper cast a disapproving glance over her untouched place setting.

Jessie clucked her tongue. 'Funny, but Ben said the same thing. Is that what love does to you?'

She gathered up the dishes and returned to the kitchen with them, leaving Keri to look thoughtfully after her. Love didn't rob you of your appetite. The destruction of love was the real robber. If only she had stuck to her vow not to become involved with Ben again, she wouldn't have this sick, empty feeling inside her. The memory of being in his arms with his mouth hungrily seeking hers wouldn't taunt her now.

Restlessly, she pushed her chair back from the table. She couldn't do anything to assuage that emptiness now. It would be with her until time healed the worst of the hurt. But perhaps she could do something about Rick's plans.

Going into Ben's office, she closed the door behind her and picked up his telephone. Within minutes she was talking to an efficient-sounding secretary who put her through as soon as she identified herself.

'Keri, how nice of you to call,' came Theo's enthusiastic response.

'It's good to talk to you, too, Theo,' she said evenly. 'I trust you enjoyed your dinner at Kinga Downs.'

'It was a memorable evening,' he confirmed, then chuckled softly. 'I trust Ben Champion wasn't too put out by my unsubtle teasing?'

'A bit, but he soon got over it,' she said truthfully, thinking that Theo's efforts to make Ben jealous were all for nothing. 'I was calling about something else. Your plan to build a casino on Casuarina land.'

She waited for him to deny that he had any such plans, but he said, 'I take it Rick has explained the project to you.'

'He didn't explain anything. He gloated about what he was going to do,' she said miserably. 'Theo, how could you be a part of this? You saw Ben's egg-ranching project for yourself. A casino would destroy all the work he's put in on it.'

'Champion Holdings is vast. Surely he can move his crocodile farm elsewhere?'

Tiredly, she explained to Theo, as she had done to Rick, how long it would take to start the project again in a new location. 'To say nothing of the eggs and animals we'd lose during the trauma of the move,' she finished.

There was silence for a moment, then Theo said, 'I'm sorry, Keri, I didn't know my choice of this site would cause you such concern. I wish there was a way I could make it up to you.'

'There is. Tell Rick you can't back the development. Without your funds, he won't be able to go ahead alone.'

'It isn't that simple,' Theo explained. 'Unless I find a loophole in the paperwork, I have no grounds for pulling out. I'm sorry.'

It sounded as if he wasn't going to try. 'I see. Well thanks, Theo. Goodbye.'

She heard him start to add something more but she was already replacing the receiver on its cradle.

If she let him go on, he would only try to make her see why the development was the only way to go. Theo valued her good opinion, she knew, but she couldn't condone his activities this time. She wondered how Rick had managed to persuade him to be part of the project, when the Theo Strathopoulos she knew had always shown concern for the wilderness and its creatures. It was one of the things she liked about him. Used to like, she amended inwardly, feeling a surge of disappointment.

There was a slim chance she could stop the development, but she balked at taking it. If Ben found out, he would never believe it wasn't another attack on Rick's wedding plans.

She felt the corners of her mouth edge up into a bitter smile. Since he already believed it, she had nothing more to lose. And the environment had everything to gain.

Loading her four-wheel-drive vehicle with supplies for a long drive took very little time. Jessie and Robyn were both preoccupied with their work, so no one saw her drive off. She wouldn't have told anyone where she was going, but basic survival in the bush demanded that someone know her destination and expected time of arrival, so she left a message on the computer for Robyn to find when she finished work.

Fortunately, she knew the area well enough to know which of the maze of unmade roads led towards Red River Homestead. As a teenager staying at Kinga Downs she had been there years ago when she and the Champion family had attended Persia Redshaw's eighteenth birthday party.

Soon afterwards, Persia had gone to Switzerland to attend an expensive finishing school and Keri hadn't seen her since. What was she like now, she wondered? In the driving mirror, she saw her mouth tighten. What she really meant was, what kind of woman would consider marrying Rick Champion?

The drive took several hours and by the time Red River homestead came into sight, Keri was worn out from battling with the heavy vehicle over the tortuous roads. She trusted to luck that Persia would be at home, not wanting to explain her mission over the telephone in advance.

Luck was with her. The woman who appeared on the front veranda to watch Keri drive up was Persia herself. She came out to the car as soon as Keri had parked it. 'This is a surprise. I wasn't expecting visitors.' She stopped in her tracks, her hand extended. 'Keri Donovan? It is you?'

'It's me,' Keri agreed, shaking the other woman's hand. 'I didn't think you'd remember me, Miss Redshaw. It's been a long time.'

'My eighteenth birthday,' Persia confirmed, proving that her memory was indeed sound. 'Call me Perry, won't you? I got sick to death of Persia and Miss Redshaw in Switzerland. Only my mother insists on my full name these days.'

Keri could hardly believe her ears. Persia was still the same porcelain-pretty doll of a woman she remembered, with candyfloss blonde hair and impossibly blue eyes, but she sounded so sensible and approachable. How on earth had she got mixed up with Rick?

At Persia's invitation, she followed the other woman into the house, welcoming its dim coolness after the heat of the day outside. Like Kinga Downs, Red River was a century-old homestead surrounded by a cluster of other buildings. It was framed by a gracious veranda with a sloping corrugated roof. The village-like atmosphere was accentuated by a clay tennis court and swimming-pool beyond which Keri glimpsed an inviting fern grotto. It was plain to see that Persia wasn't marrying Rick for his money.

Persia—Perry—rang for tea which was brought by a strikingly beautiful part-aboriginal housemaid. When they had drunk some and sampled the scones which were served with it, Perry leaned forwards. 'Now what brings you to Red River? I hope it wasn't to see my folks, because they're away at a christening in Darwin.'

Keri shook her head. 'I came to see you, actually.'

Perry nodded. 'That was kind of you. I've had half the district calling in since I got back.'

Guiltily, Keri remembered the Redshaws' recent loss which had slipped her mind until now. 'I was sorry to hear about your grandmother,' she offered belatedly. 'I lost mine a couple of years ago and it's still a dreadful shock, even when they're very old, as she was.'

Perry's eyes grew misty. 'I know. My gran was special to me, too. I'm glad I could spend those last weeks with her and Rick didn't mind postponing our wedding too much. How is he? I haven't seen much of him since I got back. He tells me they're flat-out with the cattle muster.'

Keri almost choked on her buttered scone. 'I haven't seen much of him either, because of the muster, I suppose,' she added. Now she knew how Perry could consider marrying him. He had fooled her as thoroughly as he had tried to fool Keri when she was a naïve teenager. Perry evidently thought he was the dedicated, hard-working property-owner. She recalled Rick saying they didn't know each other very well. It explained a lot.

Persia nodded understandingly. 'Ben must be caught up in it too. He'll be so relieved when Rick can take over some of the responsibility. Rick explained to me how his father's death nearly destroyed him. He couldn't face going home to Kinga Downs at first, so he travelled around trying to come to terms with himself. But you must know all this already, being engaged to Ben.' Her smile widened. 'Do you realise, that will make us sisters-in-law?'

'It will, won't it?' Keri agreed absently. Keri and Perry. They sounded more like a comedy act than potential sisters. She was stunned by how completely Rick had misled his future wife. Jake's death hadn't destroyed him at all, unless it was because the terms of the will had left Rick out in the cold. His free-spending travels had nothing to do with recovering from any grief. But Persia obviously believed the tale and it wasn't Keri's place to disillusion her, no matter what Ben expected of her. She took a deep breath. 'I did have a reason for coming here today.'

Persia gave her an expectant look. 'I'm listening.'

As directly as she could, Keri described the plans Theo and Rick had made to develop a tract of

Casuarina land into a tourist resort. 'They intend to
put a casino on the river bank, beside Ben's
crocodile farm,' she concluded.

Persia refilled her coffee-cup and held out the pot
to Keri. When she shook her head, Persia set the pot
down and sipped her drink thoughtfully. 'I see. I
had no idea what he had in mind for Casuarina.'

Keri sat forward. 'But you can see the harm it will
do to the environment?'

Long lashes fluttered down over Persia's wide
blue eyes. 'I suppose so, but it is Rick's land. Surely
he can do what he wants with it?'

Frustration welled up inside Keri, but she held it
carefully in check. 'You're right, of course. But your
childrens' future is at stake as well. Surely you don't
want them to inherit a ravaged land?'

Unexpectedly, Persia's face darkened. 'Maybe
they won't want the land at all. I grew up here with
the heat, the dust and the flies, yet I'm expected to
love it and be content with it for the rest of my life.
But I'm not.'

'I don't follow you.' But she was very much afraid
she did.

A hard glitter sprang to Persia's eyes and she
blinked rapidly. 'Why should you? I haven't told
anyone how I feel. But the truth is, I wish I'd stayed
in Switzerland when I had the chance.'

Understanding began to dawn on Keri. 'Did you
meet someone while you were over there?'

Persia wavered, as if deciding whether or not to
answer. Then she gave a deep sigh. 'I've said this
much, you may as well know the rest. It doesn't
matter now anyway.'

'I won't say anything, I promise,' Keri encouraged her.

'I met a French banker who lives permanently in Zurich. We fell in love and he wanted me to stay in Europe. Mum and Dad would die if they knew. All their lives, they've dreamed of me marrying a local man and carrying on the family traditions.'

'I take it they approve of Rick Champion?' Keri speculated aloud.

Persia's laugh was brittle. 'Oh, sure. He's tailor-made. Plenty of land, a good family name, and, for my sake, not too repulsive to look at.'

'Is that enough for marriage?' To Keri it sounded more like a shopping-list.

A shrug lifted Persia's fine-boned shoulders. 'It has to be. Dad has serious angina. I can't please myself if it's going to kill him, can I?'

There was nothing Keri could say. It was clear now why Persia intended to marry a man she didn't love, and who didn't care for her, except as a ticket to financial freedom. To Persia, if she couldn't marry her French banker, one man was as good as another, provided her parents were satisfied.

Keri felt her heart go out to the other woman. Her own parents had encouraged her to live her own life, never expecting her to fit their mould. It was difficult to understand the kind of pressure Persia felt herself under.

Still, she had to try one last time. 'Won't you at least talk to Rick about the development? You might make him think about the consequences.'

'Sound advice I could give to you as well,' came a deep masculine voice, intruding between them.

She started, astonished to find Ben framed in the doorway. She had been so engrossed in her talk with Persia that neither of them had heard his car drive up.

Persia jumped to her feet. 'Come in, Ben. Join us for tea.'

With a smooth gesture, Ben swept his Akubra hat off his head and tossed it on to the arm of a chair, then sat down and took the cup Persia handed to him. 'I knocked, but you didn't seem to hear me.'

'It's not surprising. I was telling Keri about my experiences in Switzerland and we got carried away.' The look she directed at Keri implored her to keep Persia's confidences to herself.

Over the rim of his cup, Ben's eyes met Keri's, his look accusing. 'Funny, I thought I heard you mention Rick as I came in.'

'Oh, that. Keri told me about his plans to develop Casuarina. She seemed to think I could influence him to change them.'

'Did she now.' The coolness in his voice sent a shiver down Keri's spine. She had known he would misconstrue her visit here and she thought she was prepared for the consequences. Now, his obvious condemnation stung her. 'What did you decide to do, Persia?' The question was asked idly but Keri had a feeling he was keenly interested in the answer.

'I don't know. It's his land, as I told Keri. Who knows? Maybe a casino will liven things up around here.'

'Maybe.'

'How did you get here so quickly, Ben?' Keri asked.

She knew why he had come, to stop her causing problems between Rick and Persia. He must have returned to the homestead early and read the message she had left for Robyn. But it didn't explain how he had caught up with her so quickly.

'I hitched a lift with a road train which was heading this way. I was worried about you driving all this way then having to drive back the same day, so it was a bit of luck that the trucks were coming here, wasn't it?'

'Very lucky.' She echoed his words but not the sarcasm with which they were overlaid. Now she would have to drive back to Kinga Downs in his company, since he didn't have a vehicle of his own. He knew she would consider it anything but luck, but couldn't admit it in front of Persia. Her role in the family meant they had to keep up the pretence of being happily engaged, in case word got back to Robyn before they were ready to tell her.

'I haven't congratulated you two, yet,' Persia said, missing the undercurrents between them. 'When's the happy day?'

'We haven't set a wedding day yet, have we, darling?' Ben asked, emphasising the endearment. 'But it will have to be before the dry season ends, so everyone can get here before the monsoons make the road impassable.'

Keri shot him a venomous look. Did he have to embroider the lie so much? 'Maybe we'll wait a while,' she interjected smoothly. 'After all, it was a sudden decision and we don't want to make any mistakes.' There, she had managed to plant at least a seed of doubt in Persia's mind.

'What about you and Rick?' Ben asked. 'Maybe we could arrange a double wedding.'

'Ben!' Keri cried out, appalled that he could suggest such a thing, even though she knew he was only doing it to infuriate her. He was succeeding admirably.

Persia came to the rescue. 'No, Ben. Every woman deserves her own wedding day.' Her voice sounded far away, as if she was picturing how she would have liked things to be.

Ben must have caught the wistful note in her tone. 'Is everything all right between you and Rick?'

Persia's eyes went to Keri but she shook her head imperceptibly. Persia was afraid that Ben had somehow discovered that she loved someone else. More likely, he was trying to gauge how much damage Keri had done by her visit. If only he knew the truth. 'Everything's fine,' Persia assured him. 'Why do you ask? Has Rick . . .?'

'No, Rick has said nothing to me, except how hard he's been working to get Casuarina homestead ready for the two of you.'

'That's good,' Persia sounded relieved.

'Why don't you come and see for yourself?' Ben invited. 'You and Rick haven't had much time together since you got back and Robyn would love to have you stay with us. You know how much she loves company.'

'I remember, but I promised my parents I'd keep an eye on things at Red River while they're away. I might be able to come in a few days, after they get back.'

'Sounds good to me,' Ben confirmed. 'How is

your father?'

Ben sounded as if he was aware of her father's heart problem.

'He's OK,' said Persia. 'He hates being so inactive but he hasn't the strength to work the property any more, although the nitro-glycerine pills help a lot. He's seeing a specialist while they're in Darwin, so maybe something can be done to help him.'

If it could, would Persia still feel bound to marry Rick, or would she be free to return to her banker in Switzerland, Keri wondered?

Ben gave her no chance to see Persia alone and ask her. He stood up, taking her arm, so she was forced to her feet alongside him. 'We must be going. It's a long drive back and I'd prefer to get home before dark, don't you agree, darling?'

If he called her darling once more, she would scream, she told herself. She fixed a smile to her lips and nodded. 'Of course. Thanks for the tea, Persia.'

Persia leaned closer. 'Thanks for listening to me. It's been such a relief to talk to someone. But you'll keep it to yourself, won't you?'

'I promised,' Keri reminded her, slightly irritated. If anything happened between Rick and Persia, she was bound to get the blame, yet the foundations of their relationship were already crumbling, through no fault of Keri's.

At the door, they said their goodbyes and Ben walked ahead to bring the car around to them. When he was out of earshot, Persia said, 'You're so lucky to have a man who cares about you the way Ben does. Coming all this way because he was worried about you driving back alone.' She sighed, finding the idea romantic. She wasn't to know that Ben's reasons for coming after her were anything but romantic.

As soon as they drove away from Red River homestead, he turned to her. 'What do you think you're playing at, coming out here like this?'

'You heard Persia. I wanted to talk to her about influencing Rick against the development.'

His lips tightened in condemnation. 'Against the development, or against Rick?'

She slumped, letting her seat-belt hold her upright. 'What does it matter? You'll believe what you want anyway. The fact that you came haring out here after me proves you still think you have to watch my every move.'

'Couldn't I be worried about you, for your own sake?'

The idea was so unlikely that she didn't even dignify it with an answer. Too vividly, she recalled his expression as he caught sight of the intimately placed birthmark which Rick already knew about. He would never believe she wasn't trying to win Rick back for herself.

The vehicle bumped and lurched over the rough road, making it a full-time job to remain upright. Still, Ben drove with an ease which Keri envied. He knew where he was going and could handle whatever terrain occurred along the way—in life, as well. Rough roads didn't bother him, nor rough passages in his life. He just drove roughshod over everything in his path. She sighed deeply. Right now, she was the obstacle getting in the way of his plans for his half-brother. What chance did she have of a fair hearing?

'It isn't working out the way you expected, is it?' Ben's husky voice broke into her thoughts.

She flicked her gaze sideways. 'What do you mean?'

'I spoke to Theo Strathopoulos today, about his plans for the area. I suppose you thought if you introduced Rick to Theo, he'd be so grateful that he'd fall all over you. Now it's backfired. You don't get Rick and the development goes ahead anyway.'

Her cry of protest was involuntary. 'No! It wasn't anything like that. I had no idea Theo was involved until he turned up at the crocodile farm. I wasn't hoping to buy Rick's favour, or anyone else's. Seeing this land developed is the last thing I want. I love it.'

He lifted his hands from the wheel long enough to applaud her silently. 'Convincingly put. But when I spoke to Theo this morning, he said you were the one who suggested he invest money in the Top End.'

'Yes, but in wildlife refuges and research, not casinos and resorts.'

'Maybe so, but he has his own ideas.'

'Theo always did,' she acknowledged. 'It's one of the reasons we couldn't be more than friends. He thinks men should make all the business decisions and we women should fall in with them.'

His knuckles whitened on the wheel. 'In that case, I'm sorry if I misjudged your role in this.'

'You did,' she confirmed quietly. 'I would never be a party to the destruction of the bush. I became a ranger to preserve the wilderness, not to destroy it.'

She shot him an urgent look of appeal. 'Isn't there something you can do to stop them?'

His gaze was fixed on the horizon, as he tried to pick a path for them through the choking clouds of bulldust filming the road. 'There's nothing, I'm afraid. The land belongs to Rick unless he calls off the wedding, which I don't think he's going to do. I'm sorry, Keri.'

'I know. I'm sorry for the way things have worked out,' he amended, surprising her. 'I should have let you go that first day we met up on Crocodile Creek, instead of dragging you into this mess. I guess I was hoping . . .'

Her breath tightened in her throat. 'Yes?'

'It isn't important now. Why don't you try and get some sleep? It's a long way back and you must be tired.'

She wasn't but she was defeated by his attitude. He persisted in thinking she had come back because of Rick. Granted, everything seemed to confirm this. Rick had made sure of it. But the truth was, she had come back because of Ben. Try as she might to tell herself she didn't want any repetition of the past where he was concerned, she couldn't keep away. He was in her blood, like a tropical fever, and there was no cure for his effect on her.

Dispiritedly, she took his advice and slid lower in the seat, letting the jolting movements lull her. There was no chance of drifting off to sleep as the vehicle bumped in low gear one wheel at a time through the pandanus and into the six-foot spear grass. At times, the car disappeared and wallowed like a submarine in a sea of waving grass.

The shadows were lengthening by the time they crossed back on to Champion land, their passage watched by herds of steely-grey buffalo and the occasional pert-eared dingo which slunk off into the grass as soon as their engine approached. Once, Ben spotted some wild cattle sheltering under some low-slung bulwaddie, the spiky bush which they somehow knew put them out of reach of the stockmen. 'I'll have to send Nugget to round up that lot,' he told her when she sat up to see what was the matter.

She stretched, feeling her muscles protest at the cramped conditions. 'Have we far to go yet?'

'Another hour. We're almost at Crocodile Creek. Would you like to stop and stretch your legs?'

'Please,' she nodded eagerly. Her spine felt bruised from the continuous jolting movement.

At the creek she recognised her old campsite and bent down to brush away the ashes of her fire. It seemed an age since Ben had surprised her here and she had agreed to pretend to be engaged to him. 'I'll have to get back to work soon,' she said half to herself. 'My leave is almost up.'

'I suppose you'll be glad to get back.'

She turned as he came up behind her, watching the river over her shoulder. His nearness set her nerve-ends vibrating in sympathy and it was an effort not to lean backwards, into the shelter of his arms. 'I enjoy my work.'

'That wasn't what I asked.'

A barramundi broke the surface of the dark, mangrove-clad river below them and she watched the circles eddy out to the river's edge. Would she be glad to leave? She should be, since Ben obviously cared nothing for her. Still, she knew it would be a wrench to go, knowing that part of her would remain here with him. Like Persia, she couldn't stop loving just because the beloved was beyond reach. She could only carry on somehow, as Persia had made up her mind to do.

'You haven't answered my question.'

'I don't know the answer,' she said, her voice breaking a little. 'There's nothing to keep me here now, is there?'

His hand had been on her arm and he dropped it abruptly, turning back towards the car. 'I suppose not.'

Too late, she realised that he thought she meant Rick again. Once he was married, Ben assumed, she wouldn't want to be here.

Watching him stride back through the grass towards the car, she felt an overwhelming need to feel his arms around her once more, before she had to leave. 'Ben, wait,' she called as she hurried up the bank after him.

By the time she reached the car, he was no longer alone. With him was Nugget Malone. He had evidently ridden out from the homestead at speed because his horse's flanks were pumping and white-flecked. 'What's the matter?' she asked, forgetting her own worries as anxiety overtook her. Something bad must have happened at home to bring Nugget out here in such a hurry.

Nugget twisted his bush hat between long, bony fingers. 'It's Robyn. This afternoon she started having some trouble breathing. We managed to get the doctor on the radio and he told us what to do. She's all right now, really,' he assured a white-faced Keri.

'But the doctor's on his way?' Ben asked.

'Yes, Ben. His plane landed an hour ago. I made sure he had everything he needed before I set off to find you. I knew you'd want to get back as quick as you could.'

'You did the right thing,' Ben assured him. 'You go ahead. We'll follow as fast as we can.'

'I was afraid that Theo's offer would be too much for her,' she said as they started off again. This time, Ben drove as fast as the terrain allowed, with little heed for the effect on the occupants. Keri knew she would have bruises all over her body by the time they got back. It didn't matter now. What mattered was that Robyn should be all right.

'What offer?' Ben asked over the clattering of the car's gears.

She explained about Theo wanting to buy the entire Escarpment series of paintings. 'He didn't know she couldn't have any excitement,' she explained.

'I wasn't blaming him,' Ben said, his eyes fixed on the road. 'If anyone's to blame, it's me for leaving her alone when I knew how touchy things were.'

If she hadn't gone off to see Persia, Ben wouldn't have left the homestead either, Keri thought. Now Ben had yet another grievance against her to add to his list.

Gripping the sides of the bucking vehicle with grim determination, she knew they couldn't go on like this. The sooner she left Kinga Downs, the better for all of them.

CHAPTER TEN

AS soon as she saw Doctor Syme's grave expression on their return to Kinga Downs, Keri knew she wouldn't be leaving for some time yet. The doctor looked grey-faced and tired, a far cry from the jovial medico Keri remembered meeting at Robyn's party.

'Is she all right?' Ben asked for both of them.

'She's holding her own,' he said grimly. 'It's a good thing you people keep oxygen equipment here or I would have had to risk flying her out to a hospital.'

'Oh, no,' Keri gasped. 'What's the matter with her?'

The doctor patted her hand reassuringly. 'Don't look so stricken, the worst is over now, thank goodness. Being so run down, she picked up a lung infection and it affected her breathing. After a few hours on oxygen, she should be all right. I've given her something to treat the infection.'

'Then she won't have to be taken to hospital?'

'Not unless she takes a turn for the worse. I'm going to stick around overnight if you folks don't mind.'

'I've already made up a guest suite,' Jessie supplied even as Ben opened his mouth. He nodded.

'Stay as long as you need to, Doctor. I'm sure Rob will be happier under her own roof.'

'Precisely why I intend to keep her here if I can,'

the doctor agreed. 'Her morale is as vital to her recovery as antibiotics.' Excusing himself, the doctor went back to his patient with Jessie following him, clucking like a mother hen.

When they had gone, Keri collasped into a chair. 'I guess I shouldn't think of leaving yet.'

Ben gave her a sharp look. 'You heard what Doctor Syme said about Robyn's morale. It would drop like a stone if we told her the truth about our engagement now.'

She couldn't keep the bitterness out of her voice. 'Do you think I don't know that? I would have called a halt to this charade long ago if it hadn't been for Robyn.'

'I see,' he said quietly.

She doubted it, however. He couldn't see how it tore at her to have to pretend to be in love with him and have him think it was all an act.

The dust had collected in the crevices of his face so that he looked like a granite carving, given life. He massaged his eyes with one dust-streaked hand. 'I may have to ask more of you yet.'

What new torment could he devise for her now? 'Yes?' she asked uncuriously.

'I want to tell Robyn we've set the wedding date, maybe even let her start planning the whole affair.'

Her eyes widened in shock. 'You can't be serious? It will only make matters worse when she has to learn the truth.'

'Perhaps. But in the meantime it would give her an incentive to get well. If she suspects that something's wrong, she may lose hope altogether.'

'I've told you I'm willing to go on with our act.'

'But it may not be enough. She'll think it strange if we don't start making plans. She may even work it out for herself. You wouldn't want that, would you?'

'I suppose not,' she conceded with a heavy heart. What kind of a monster would she be if she refused? 'All right, you can tell her what you like and I won't contradict you.'

'Not good enough,' he said shortly. 'You have to show some enthusiasm for the whole idea.'

'Do you know what you're asking of me?' She was sure he had no idea.

'I know. I'm asking you to pretend to love someone you can't stand, after I came between you and Rick. But I promise you it won't be for much longer, just until Robyn is well.'

Just until Robyn is well. How often was she given cause to regret those words in the days which followed? In front of Robyn, she was forced to act the part of the blushing bride, while her friend keyed into her computer lists of flowers, food and ceremonies which Keri knew would never be needed.

Ben had been right, though. The plan did have a positive effect on his sister. Two days after her collapse, the doctor had discontinued the oxygen treatment, and now Robyn was able to sit up in bed and eat a little solid good.

She tired quickly, but defied the doctor's orders to rest, preferring to throw what little energy she had into plans for the wedding.

'I'm worried about her doing so much,' Keri confided to Doctor Syme after one such planning session.

'Don't worry, this is the best therapy she could have,' the doctor assured her. His eyes twinkled. 'Just don't call the whole thing off and give her a relapse, will you?'

His comment, so unknowingly near to the truth, sent a shaft of pain darting through Keri. Ben thought she was being heroic, going through all this for Robyn's sake. He couldn't know the agony it cost her to plan a wedding to the man she loved, knowing it would never take place.

Ben played his part to the hilt, acting the loving fiancée in front of Robyn as if he really meant it. If she hadn't known better, Keri would have sworn his kisses were genuine, as his lips sought hers with insistent warmth until she felt dizzy with the need to feel his arms around her for real.

When she thought she could stand it no longer, Doctor Symes announced that Robyn had made sufficient progress for him to visit weekly instead of daily. 'Don't forget, I want an invitation to the wedding,' he reminded her as he left.

Keri crushed the list she had been holding between her fists. If only there were a wedding to invite him to, and she could look forward to living happily ever after as Ben's wife. But they both knew it was a charade and would soon be over. If only it didn't hurt so much to think about it.

She had hardly seen Rick since Robyn's collapse. His visits to his sister had been infrequent and Keri had taken care not to be alone with him, to avoid giving Ben any more ammunition against her.

So she was surprised when he stormed in unannounced one afternoon and all but hauled her to her feet. 'This is your doing, Miss Know-all,' he swore, thrusting a piece of paper under her nose.

Startled, she backed away. 'I don't know what you mean, Rick.'

'Oh no? Then tell me you didn't go and visit Persia Redshaw and meddle in our affairs.'

'I did go to see her,' she admitted, still confused. 'But I didn't meddle, as you put it. We talked about the development, that's all.'

'And you convinced her it was a terrible thing, didn't you?'

'No, I didn't. She was in favour of it, as it happened. I couldn't persuade her to change her mind. She was on your side,' she repeated, wanting him to understand her clearly.

'That's not the way I read this,' he said, shaking the paper at her again. 'Read it for yourself.'

It fluttered to the ground at her feet and she picked it up with shaking fingers. When she began to read it silently, he insisted she read it aloud. 'Dear Rick,' she began then looked up as her eye fell on the signature at the bottom. 'It's personal, Rick. Are you sure you want me to read it?'

'I want you to see the harm you've done with your interfering,' he said.

With an effort, she managed to steady her breathing and read the letter aloud. 'Dear Rick, I'm sorry I don't have the courage to tell you this to your face. My father has undergone heart surgery for his angina and is making a splendid recovery. He should be back to full health in a few weeks.' She looked up, smiling. 'Surely that's good news, Rick?'

'Go on,' he urged. 'You haven't got to the best part yet.'

Puzzled, she read on. 'As soon as my father recovers, we shall be travelling to Europe on an extended holiday. I shall be taking my parents to Switzerland to meet some friends I made while I was at school there. One of them is a man I came to care for very deeply. It is him I wish to marry, so I am returning your ring. I am sorry to bring you this news but I could not have been a good wife to you when my heart was elsewhere. Thank you for your patience and understanding, Persia.'

When she looked up, Rick was glaring at her. 'You still don't understand, do you?'

'Of course I'm sorry about your wedding, but you admitted you didn't love her. What else is there to say?'

'You're forgetting brother Ben's terms. No wife, no land,' he growled. 'Now do you see what you've done?'

She let the letter drop to the floor. 'I didn't do anything, Rick. Persia loves someone else. It had nothing to do with my visit. She was in love with him before I went near her.'

'But she wasn't going to do anything about it until you showed up.' His mouth twisted into an ugly smile. 'I'll bet you gave her some sisterly advice about following her heart.'

Keri's temper snapped. 'She couldn't do any such thing as long as her father was ill. It would have killed him to know she was in love with a man from another country. She couldn't say anything until he was well.'

Rick ground the letter under his heel. 'You have an answer for everything, don't you? Well, let's see you answer this one. The bulldozers are already starting work on the Crocodile Creek site. By the time Ben finds out the wedding's off, it will be too late to halt the development and I'll have won anyway.'

He left her standing open mouthed, shaking with the shock of what he had just told her. Surely he was bluffing? He couldn't have started work on the casino site without clear title to the land? If only she could get in touch with Ben, but he was out on the property somewhere. He wouldn't be home until sundown. And she couldn't leave Robyn alone in the house until Jessie got back from her Country Womens' Association meeting. There had to be something she could do.

The clutter around her feet caught her eye and she looked at the label she had been writing when Rick came in. She had been packing the last of Robyn's paintings to ship to Theo and the label with his address lay at her feet. Picking it up, she went to the telephone.

'Please be there, please be there,' she repeated to herself as his number began to ring.

His secretary told her he was in a meeting but reluctantly agreed to disturb him when Keri insisted that the matter was urgent.

'What is it, Keri, you sound upset,' said Theo when he answered the phone at last.

'I am, and I'm sorry to take you away from your meeting, but I need your help.' She went on to explain Rick's visit and ended by asking him to halt further work on the project until Ben could be informed.

At the other end of the line, there was a long silence punctuated by Theo's laboured breathing. 'I wish I could help you, my dear, but there's nothing I can do,' he said, his tone gentle.

'You mean because they've already started?' she asked, hearing herself sounding shrill and on the verge of losing control.

'No, no. Calm yourself,' he said urgently. 'You can't do anything because I'm not involved. After your last call, I looked more closely at the project and decided that you were right. The outback needs a crocodile farm more than it needs another casino. I had my lawyers find me that loophole.'

'Oh, Theo, I should have had more faith in you,' she said. 'I'm sorry I jumped to the wrong conclusion.'

'But it was partly the right one,' he intervened. 'If work has already started on clearing the site, Rick must have found another backer for his project, so you are no better off.'

'Yes, I am,' she assured him. 'This way, whatever happens I haven't lost a friend.'

It was a wonderful discovery but it didn't solve the immediate problem, she realised as she hung up the telephone. She was immeasurably relieved that Theo wasn't involved in the destruction of Casuarina, but evidently someone else was, probably another of the financial wizards Rick knew in Darwin. There was no shortage of people to whom wilderness was less important than development. Rick wouldn't have had to look far.

Whoever it was must have accepted Rick's word that Casuarina belonged to him, and was willing to start work on the strength of it. By the time their mistake was pointed out, it might be too late to save the property from destruction.

In an agony of indecision, Keri paced up and down, scattering the packing material for Robyn's pictures as she paced. Fortunately, Robyn was asleep. The last thing she needed was to be burdened with this problem when she was starting to get well.

Then the sound of the front door opening and closing announced that Jessie Finch was back. Thanking her stars that the housekeeper hadn't chosen this particular day to linger with her friends at the CWA, Keri ran up and flung her arms around the startled woman. 'I'm so glad to see you.'

'I wasn't gone that long,' Jessie said, laughing. 'Is Robyn all right?'

'She's fine. She slept most of the afternoon.' Keri looked around at the mess she was leaving behind. 'Don't worry about all this, I'll finish the job and clear up when I get back.'

'Get back from where?' Jessie asked, bewildered.

'Crocodile Creek,' Keri flung over her shoulder as she hurtled out of the door.

The dusty track to the crocodile farm seemed endless as she bumped and jerked her way along in low gear, the wheels plunging in and out of pot-holes until she felt like a rodeo rider trying to stay on a bucking brumby. Mobs of doe-eyed buffaloes watched her pass from under the sparse shade of gum trees and lancewoods.

At last she drove between the sliprails marking the entrance to the reserve. A sense of relief swamped her. Instead of the roar of land-clearing equipment, she heard only the chirrup of cicadas and the monotonous drone of mosquitoes along the riverbank. Maybe Rick had been bluffing after all.

There was no one around as she approached the pens holding Ben's crocodiles. Most of the smaller animals lay unmoving in the sun, half in and half out of their pools. Not an eye blinked as she passed the pens but she knew that her movements were marked. Without the reinforced wire fencing, she would have been dragged into a pool in an instant.

The thought made her shiver as she reached Fang's pen. There was no sign of the big crocodile but a careful search of the lilies thronging the surface of the water revealed two dark nodules, Fang's nostrils as he came up for air. Then she drew a sharp breath as she noticed a jagged tear in the wire netting which separated Fang's pen from Matilda's. She rushed to Matilda's pen and peered over the fence.

She let out the breath she had been holding as she caught sight of the female crocodile, her body S-bent around a tree, and her long tail trailing into the water. 'What have you two been up to?' she asked the motionless creature.

Matilda's eyelid lowered fractionally. She was chasing flies from her eyes but it looked uncannily like a wink. Keri cast a professional eye around the dense grass and sedges surrounding her pool. Sure enough, she spotted several mounds of vegetation dug along the bank and felt a thrill of excitement as she recognised the trial nests Matilda had been building. No one knew why crocodiles built such nests weeks before they laid their eggs, unless it was to make sure that the site finally chosen was sufficiently moist to protect the eggs.

Although it was far from the first time that crocodiles had nested in captivity, Keri was proud of the achievement. She and Ben had provided Matilda with a safe, natural environment in which she felt secure enough to breed. How pleased Ben would be when she told him the news.

A throaty roar burst upon her eardrums, shattering the quiet of the riverside. Startled, she spun around to see a huge earth-moving machine rumbling into the clearing. Her joy at finding the nest turned to despair as she realised Rick hadn't been bluffing after all. He really meant to destroy this paradise.

Acting on instinct, she ran towards the machine, waving her arms and shouting at the top of her lungs. The driver couldn't hear her over the roar of his machine, but he had to see her and stop. He *had* to.

For a heart-stopping moment she thought he was going to drive right over her but he rumbled to a stop just feet away.

'What are you doing, lady?' he called down. 'Trying to get yourself killed?'

'I'm trying to stop you making an expensive mistake,' she called back. 'You have no right to clear this land.'

He pulled a piece of paper out of his pocket.

'That's not what it says here. My authority comes from Mr Champion who owns this place. He wants it cleared, I clear it.'

'I take it you mean Mr Ben Champion,' she said firmly.

He glanced at the document. 'Well, no, it says Richard Champion. Is there a difference?'

'Richard doesn't own this land. Ben does.'

Pulling out a vast square of cloth, he mopped at his face. 'Good grief! How was I to know? Are you Mrs Champion?'

She showed him her identification. 'Ranger Donovan of the Crocodile Task Force.'

At the use of her full title, he blanched. 'Jeepers. I think I'd better check this out before I do any more work.'

'I think you had, too,' agreed a masculine voice.

The bulldozer had claimed her entire attention so that she hadn't heard Ben arrive in his Range Rover. When he saw Ben approaching, the bulldozer-driver looked uncomfortable. 'Look, mister, I didn't know there were two of you.'

Ben offered the man his hand. 'Ben Champion. I'm sorry about the misunderstanding. You were only doing your job. If you call my office I'll see you're compensated for the wasted time.'

The driver accepted the card Ben offered him and started his machine up again. This time, he steered it out of the reserve and they heard it rumbling away into the distance. Ben turned to Keri. 'It looks as if I got here just in time.'

Reaction caught up with her and she began to tremble. 'Rick really meant to destroy the reserve.

When he came to the house this morning and told me what he intended to do, I was sure he was bluffing.'

'Well, he wasn't,' Ben confirmed grimly. 'Even though he had no claim to this land now Persia has returned his ring.'

Her eyes widened. 'You know about that?'

'Persia called me for advice before she wrote to Rick. That gave me time to check with my solicitor and revoke the existing agreement which gave Casuarina to Rick. I thought he might pull something like this. Next time, I'll make sure I write in a caveat against large-scale development.'

'Oh, Ben, that's wonderful news.' Before she realised what she was doing, she had thrown her arms around him in sheer joy and relief that the nightmare was over.

She was unprepared when he stiffly disengaged her arms and took a step away from her. 'I'm glad you're pleased.'

Hurt by the gesture of rejection, she said, 'Of course I'm pleased. Now your crocodile farm is safe for ever.'

'It's safe, and I'm thankful, since it's about all I have to be thankful for now.'

Her startled gaze flew to his face. 'What do you mean, Ben?'

His eyes softened then shadows claimed them again. 'Don't you know what it will be like for me, to live here and watch you and Rick build a life together on my doorstep?'

She opened her mouth to tell him how wrong he was but before she could get the words out she choked on a cloud of dust as a car barrelled up to them. Rick jumped out. 'What the hell are you doing? I passed the bulldozer on its way out of here. He's working for me, not you.'

Ben swung his attention to Rick. 'Then he's working for you somewhere else.'

'This is my land. You can't stop me clearing it.'

'Yes, I can. Persia told me she had changed her mind so I changed the conditions of the title deed. You can still have the land when you marry, but to farm, not to destroy.'

Rick glared at Keri, his hands balling into fists. 'You bitch, this is your doing, isn't it?'

Ben stepped between them. 'Don't blame Keri. God help her, she loves you.'

The admission was wrung from Ben but only elicited a hard burst of laughter from Rick. 'Loves me? That's rich, considering she's never had eyes for anyone but you.'

Ben looked at her in confusion, his eyes dark with pain. 'But the cheque, the scene in your bedroom . . .'

'Tell him the truth, Rick,' she implored.

She half expected Rick to say that they were lovers, and ruin any chance for her and Ben, but to her astonishment he said, 'What's the use? I've had my fun watching you two destroy each other.'

'Then there's nothing between the two of you?'

'There never was, Ben,' she said quietly.

Ben took a step towards his half-brother. 'Get out of here before I kill you.' He sounded as if he meant it.

Rick looked alarmed, also sensing that Ben was serious. He raised his hands defensively. 'No need to get rough. I know when I'm not wanted. But I'll need some cash to set myself up somewhere else.'

'I'll make sure you have enough money to do what you want, Rick, as long as it's far away from here,' Ben agreed.

Any other man would have salvaged his pride and refused to accept Ben's money, but Rick wasn't a fool. 'I'll write and tell you where to send the cheques,' he said and went back to his car.

Ben waited until the noise of the car engine died away then turned to Keri. 'I'm sorry. This wasn't how you wanted it to turn out, was it?'

She felt the corners of her mouth twitch into the beginnings of a smile. 'It's exactly how I wanted things to turn out.'

'But Rick's gone. You heard him, he won't be back.'

She could hardly believe he still expected her to mourn Rick's departure. 'Good,' she said, putting satisfaction into her tone.

His eyes narrowed and a gleam lit them. 'Don't play games with me, Keri. I won't settle for being second best.'

She shook her head so that the golden curls cascaded in the air, flashing brightly where the sunlight caught the strands. 'You won't have to. You see, I've finally stopped lying to myself.'

'About Rick?'

'No, he was the one doing that. I've been lying to myself and I didn't even know it. I thought I came back to prove you couldn't hurt me any more. I was wrong. You're the only man alive who can.'

'What are you trying to say? That Rick was right?

You do care for me?'

She leaned against a fence rail and spoke to the crocodile watching them behind the wire, but her words were for Ben. 'It was one of the few true things he said.' She swung around, facing him. 'Rick always wanted what you had. He thought you got everything by right of birth. He couldn't accept that you earned every single thing you have.'

'Even you?' He forced the question out in rasping tones.

She smiled shyly. 'You didn't have to work very hard at that.'

'Come here, Keri.'

It was said as an order but there was a note of desperation underlying it which drew her towards him like a magnet. In the hot sun, his body felt fiery to her tentative touch, then she was pulled into his arms and there was no more time for thinking.

All her questions vanished in the heat of his embrace as he moulded her sun-warmed body against him so that she was achingly aware of every masculine contour in his taut frame. Her hands clasped his wide shoulders and drew his head down until their lips met. According to the aborigines, devils haunted every cave and waterhole in the bush. There were devils in his kiss, too, bewitching her so that she was robbed of her power to think rationally. She could only swoop and fly with the kitehawks on currents of delicious sensation which took her to new heights of pleasure and passion.

When he drew his mouth reluctantly away from hers, he said softly, 'I love you, Ranger Donovan.'

'I love you, too, Ben Champion. I just wish it

hadn't taken us both so long to face the fact.'

'I was so sure you loved Rick,' he said raggedly.

She moved restively in the circle of his arms. 'He wanted you to think so. He couldn't stand the thought of your having everything.'

A frown creased his forehead. 'But he knew so much about you.'

She knew he was referring to the birthmark. She had no choice but to tell him the whole story, otherwise it would hang like a cloud over the rest of their days together. 'I didn't want to tell you,' she began haltingly. 'But the night I left Kinga Downs, something happened.' Her voice broke and she found, even now, that that night still hurt to think about.

'Go on,' he prompted gently.

'Rick was so mad about being left out of Jake's will that he . . . he took it out on me.'

'He raped you?' Ben's voice vibrated with fury at the very idea.

'No, he tried and he managed to rip my clothes, but I ran away from him into the bush behind the house.'

'So that's how he knew about the birthmark,' Ben observed. 'My God, did he put those marks on your shoulders, too? I swear I'll kill him after all.'

She slid a finger on to his lips, silencing his anger, then drew a strangled breath as his mouth fastened on to the finger, drawing it between his teeth. She felt his tongue curl around it, stirring a symphony of longing inside her. It was an effort to reclaim her hand. 'Let it rest, Ben. He's gone.'

'But to take a bullwhip to you, scarring you for

life. What sort of monster would do such a thing?'

This was much harder than she thought it would be. How could she tell him the truth, knowing what it must do to him? But there was no choice. She couldn't let him go on thinking Rick had scarred her. 'It wasn't Rick,' she said, her voice low. 'It was an accident. The man who did it never even knew I was hiding in the bushes.'

She felt rather than heard his cry of protest. 'Oh, lord, Keri. It was me, wasn't it? I did this to you?' Dumbly she nodded, fighting the tears which clustered behind her eyes as she witnessed the depths of his pain.

'It was an accident,' she repeated hoarsely.

'I remember now. I was practising for the whip-cracking championship. I held the state title then. I felt the whip strike something soft but I thought it was an animal or something. When I searched the bushes, I found nothing.'

'I'd gone back to my room by then,' she breathed. 'I didn't blame you. How could I? I loved you.'

'Even after I'd hurt you?'

'You didn't know. And I hurt you, too, in a way, by not living up to your expectations.'

'Damn my expectations,' he countered. 'If I hadn't been so blind, we could have been together all this time and I wouldn't have had to read about you in the newspapers like a lovesick fool.'

It was hard to imagine Ben being a fool over anything, even love, and she thrilled to the knowledge that she held such sway with him. 'I should have guessed what was going on when you remembered all those stories,' she observed.

He grinned wryly. 'I told myself I was only reading them out of curiosity. But curiosity doesn't make you feel murderous reading about your girl dating a millionaire.'

'But I didn't know I was yours then.'

'You know it now, don't you?' he asked anxiously. 'Why do you think I was so keen to get a ring on your finger? I didn't want to take a chance on your escaping from me a second time.'

'So it wasn't all for Rick?' she asked, feeling a sensation of warmth steal over her.

He frowned. 'I wanted to keep my promise to my father, but I needed to keep you here for myself, too.'

'Even though I disappointed you before?' she asked, recalling his earlier admission. She hadn't guessed that she was the woman he had been describing.

He shook his head. 'You never disappointed me. You were always honest with me, more than I was with myself, it seems.' His arms tightened around her. 'I swear I'll make it up to you, my darling. I'll never hurt you again as long as I live.'

She nestled into the circle of his embrace, murmuring in contentment. 'Is this a proposal, Mr Champion.'

His lips grazed the top of her head. 'You bet it is. You can hardly be surprised since I've been pushing you towards a wedding for ages, with Robyn's help.'

'I wish I'd known you were serious,' she confessed. 'It would have made all the difference.'

'As long as it makes a difference now,' he said. 'You seemed so anxious to get away that it was the

only way I could keep you here. I thought I was
going to have to set a trap for you, as we did for
Fang.'

'I only wanted to get away because you didn't
seem to care,' she told him. 'The truth is, you don't
need a snare. You caught me a long time ago.'

Accepting the invitation of her parted lips, he
showered her with tiny kisses. 'This time,' he said as
his mouth moved over hers, 'I don't mean to let you
go.'

She smiled teasingly. 'Just try it.'

In answer, he pulled her close against him, setting
the blood singing in her veins and triggering a
craving which she knew would only be satisfied by
the fulfilment of his possession. The thought
heightened her responses and she matched his kisses
with equal ardour. His warm breath on her mouth
was like a promise of life and she drank it in eagerly.

In the background, she heard Fang's throaty roar
as the male crocodile called to his mate. Suddenly it
seemed as if the entire outback resounded with the
calls of love.

Harlequin Romance

Coming Next Month

#3007 BLUEPRINT FOR LOVE Amanda Clark
Shannon West knows that renovating an old house means
uncovering its hidden strengths. When she meets Griff Marek,
an embittered architect—and former sports celebrity—she
learns that love can do the same thing.

#3008 HEART OF MARBLE Helena Dawson
Cressida knows it's risky taking a job sight unseen, but Sir Piers
Aylward's offer to help him open Clarewood Priory to the
public is too good to miss. Then she discovers that he wants
nothing to do with the planning—or with her.

#3009 TENDER OFFER Peggy Nicholson
Did Clay McCann really think he could cut a path through
Manhattan, seize her father's corporation—and her—without a
fight? Apparently he did! And Rikki wondered what had
happened to the Clay she'd idolized in her teens.

#3010 NO PLACE LIKE HOME Leigh Michaels
Just when Kaye's dreams are within reach—she's engaged to a
kind, gentle man who's wealthy enough to offer real security—
happy-go-lucky Brendan McKenna shows up, insisting that *he's*
the only man who can really bring her dreams to life....

#3011 TO STAY FOREVER Jessica Steele
Kendra travels to Greece without hesitation to answer her
cousin Faye's call for help. And Eugene, Faye's husband, seems
grateful. Not so his associate, Damon Niarkos, the most hateful
man Kendra's ever met. What right does he have to interfere?

#3012 RISE OF AN EAGLE Margaret Way
Morgan's grandfather Edward Hartland had always encouraged
the enmity between her and Tyson—yet in his will he divided
the Hartland empire between them. Enraged, Morgan tries to
convince Ty that he's a usurper in her home!

Available in October wherever paperback books are sold, or
through Harlequin Reader Service:

In the U.S.
901 Fuhrmann Blvd.
P.O. Box 1397
Buffalo, N.Y. 14240-1397

In Canada
P.O. Box 603
Fort Erie, Ontario
L2A 5X3

ℋ𝑎𝑟𝑙𝑒𝑞𝑢𝑖𝑛 𝐴𝑚𝑒𝑟𝑖𝑐𝑎𝑛 𝑅𝑜𝑚𝑎𝑛𝑐𝑒®

SUMMER.

The sun, the surf, the sand...

One relaxing month by the sea was all Zoe, Diana and Gracie ever expected from their four-week stays at Gull Cottage, the luxurious East Hampton mansion. They never thought they'd soon be sharing those long summer days—or hot summer nights—with a special man. They never thought that what they found at the beach would change their lives forever. But as Boris, Gull Cottage's resident mynah bird said: ''Beware of summer romances....''

Join Zoe, Diana and Gracie for the summer of their lives. Don't miss the GULL COTTAGE trilogy in American Romance: #301 *Charmed Circle* by Robin Francis (July 1989), #305 *Mother Knows Best* by Barbara Bretton (August 1989) and #309 *Saving Grace* by Anne McAllister (September 1989).

GULL COTTAGE—because a month can be the start of forever...

Harlequin Regency Romance™

Romance the way it was *always* meant to be!

The time is 1811, when a Regent Prince rules the empire. The place is London, the glittering capital where rakish dukes and dazzling debutantes scheme and flirt in a dangerously exciting game. Where marriage is the passport to wealth and power, yet every girl hopes secretly for love....

Welcome to Harlequin Regency Romance where reading is an adventure and romance is *not* just a thing of the past! Two delightful books a month.

Available wherever Harlequin Books are sold.

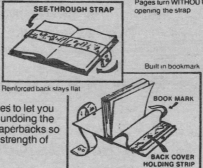

COMING SOON...

Indulge a Little
Give a Lot

An irresistible opportunity to pamper
yourself with free* gifts and help a
great cause, Big Brothers/Big Sisters
Programs and Services.
*With proofs-of-purchase plus postage and handling.

Watch for it in October!

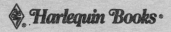